Childhood and Other Neighborhoods

About the Author

Born and raised on the southwest side of Chicago, Stuart Dybek is the author of three short story collections, *Childhood and Other Neighborhoods*, *The Coast of Chicago*, and *I Sailed with Magellan*, as well as two collections of poetry, *Brass Knuckles* and *Streets in Their Own Ink*. His award-winning poetry and fiction have appeared in numerous magazines, including *The New Yorker*, *The Atlantic Monthly*, *Harper's*, *The Iowa Review*, *Antæus*, and *Ploughshares*.

Childhood and Other Neighborhoods

STORIES

Stuart Dybek

The University of Chicago Press

The University of Chicago Press, Chicago, 60637
 First published 1980
University of Chicago Press edition 2003
Printed in the United States of America
12 11 10 09 08 07 06 05 04   2 3 4 5

ISBN: 0-226-17658-4 (paper)

Acknowledgments:

City Lights: From *Howl and Other Poems* by Allen Ginsberg. Copyright © 1956, 1959 by Allen Ginsberg. Reprinted by permission of City Lights Books.

Houghton Mifflin Company: From *Duino Elegies and Sonnets to Orpheus*, by Rainer Maria Rilke, translated by A. Poulin, Jr. Copyright © 1975, 1976, 1977 by A. Poulin, Jr. Reprinted by permission of Houghton Mifflin Company and Insel Verlag.

Some of these stories originally appeared in the following: *Antæus, Chicago Review, Commonweal, The Falcon, The Iowa Review, The Magazine of Fantasy and Science Fiction*, and *Northwest Review*.

Library of Congress Cataloging-in-Publication Data

Dybek, Stuart, 1942–
Childhood and other neighborhoods : stories / by Stuart Dybek.
p. cm.
Contents: The Palatski man—The cat woman—Blood soup—Neighborhood drunk—Visions of Budhardin—The long thoughts—The wake—Sauerkraut soup—Charity—Horror movie—The apprentice.
ISBN 0-226-17658-4 (pbk. : alk. paper)
1. Chicago (Ill.)—Fiction. I. Title.

PS3554 .Y3C5 2003
813′.54—dc21   2003051398

⊗The paper used in this publication meets the minimum requirements of the American National Standard for Information Sciences-Permanence of Paper for Printed Library Materials, ANSI Z39.48-1992.

for my mother and father

Contents

Who'll show a child just as he is? Who'll set
him in his constellation and put the measure
of distance in his hand? Who'll make the death
of a child out of gray bread growing hard—or
leave it there in his round mouth like the core
of a sweet apple . . . ?

—Rainer Maria Rilke

Childhood and
Other Neighborhoods

The Palatski Man

He reappeared in spring, some Sunday morning, perhaps Easter, when the twigs of the catalpa trees budded and lawns smelled of mud and breaking seeds. Or Palm Sunday, returning from mass with handfuls of blessed, bending palms to be cut into crosses and pinned on your Sunday dress and the year-old palms removed by her brother, John, from behind the pictures of Jesus with his burning heart and the Virgin with her sad eyes, to be placed dusty and crumbling in an old coffee can and burned in the backyard. And once, walking back from church, Leon Sisca said these are what they lashed Jesus with. And she said no they aren't, they used whips. They used these, he insisted. What do you know, she said. And he told her she was a dumb girl and lashed her across her bare legs with his blessed palms. They stung her; she started to cry, that anyone could do such a thing, and he caught her running down Twenty-fifth Street with her skirt flying and got her against a fence, and grabbing her by the hair, he stuck his scratchy palms in her face, and suddenly he was lifted off the ground and flung to the sidewalk, and she saw John standing over him very red in the face; and when Leon Sisca tried to run away, John blocked him, and Leon tried to dodge around him as if they were playing football; and as he cut past, John slapped him across the face; Leon's head snapped back and his nose started to bleed. John didn't chase him and he ran halfway down the block, turned around and yelled through his tears with blood dripping on his white shirt: I hate you goddamn you I hate you! All the dressed-up people coming back from church saw it happen and shook their heads. John said c'mon Mary let's go home.

No, it wasn't that day, but it was in that season on a Sunday that he reappeared, and then every Sunday after that through the summer and into the fall, when school would resume and the green catalpa leaves fall like withered fans into the birdbaths, turning the water brown, the Palatski Man would come.

He was an old man who pushed a white cart through the neighborhood streets ringing a little golden bell. He would stop at each corner, and the children would come with their money to inspect the taffy apples sprinkled with chopped nuts, or the red candy apples on pointed sticks, or the *palatski* displayed under the glass of the white cart. She had seen taffy apples in the candy stores and even the red apples sold by clowns at circuses, but she had never seen *palatski* sold anywhere else. It was two crisp wafers stuck together with honey. The taste might have reminded you of an ice-cream cone spread with honey, but it reminded Mary of Holy Communion. It felt like the Eucharist in her mouth, the way it tasted walking back from the communion rail after waiting for Father Mike to stand before her wearing his rustling silk vestments with the organ playing and him saying the Latin prayer over and over faster than she could ever hope to pray and making a sign of the cross with the host just before placing it on someone's tongue. She knelt at the communion rail close enough to the altar to see the silk curtains drawn inside the open tabernacle and the beeswax candles flickering and to smell the flowers. Father Mike was moving down the line of communicants, holding the chalice, with the altar boy, an eighth-grader, sometimes even John, standing beside him in a lace surplice, holding the paten under each chin; and she would close her eyes and open her mouth, sticking her tongue out, and hear the prayer and feel the host placed gently on her tongue. Sometimes Father's hand brushed her bottom lip, and she would feel a spark from his finger, which Sister said was static electricity, not the Holy Spirit.

Then she would walk down the aisle between the lines of communicants, searching through half-shut eyes for her pew, her mind praying Jesus help me find it. And when she found her pew, she would kneel down and shut her eyes and bury her face in her hands praying over and over thank you Jesus for coming to me, feeling the host stuck to the roof of her mouth, melting against her tongue like a warm, wheaty snowflake; and she would turn the tip of her tongue inward and lick the host off the ridges of her mouth till it was loosened by saliva and swallowed into her soul.

Who was the Palatski Man? No one knew or even seemed to care. He was an old man with an unremembered face, perhaps a never-seen face, a head hidden by a cloth-visored cap, and eyes concealed behind dark glasses with green, smoked lenses. His smile revealed only a gold crown and a missing tooth. His only voice was the ringing bell, and his hands were rough and red as if scrubbed with sandpaper and their skin very hard when you opened your hand for your change and his fingers brushed yours. His clothes were always the same—white—not starched and dazzling, but the soft white of many washings and wringings.

No one cared and he was left alone. The boys didn't torment him as they did the peddlers during the week. There was constant war between the boys and the peddlers, the umbrella menders, the knife sharpeners, anyone whose business carried him down the side streets or through the alleys. The peddlers came every day, spring, summer, and autumn, through the alleys behind the backyard fences crying, "Rags ol irn, rags ol irn!" Riding their ancient, rickety wagons with huge wooden-spoked wheels, heaped high with scraps of metal, frames of furniture, coal-black cobwebbed lumber, bundles of rags and filthy newspapers. The boys called them the Ragmen. They were all old, hunched men, bearded and bald, who bargained in a stammered foreign English and dressed in clothes extracted from the bundles of rags in their weather-beaten wagons.

Their horses seemed even more ancient than their masters, and Mary was always sorry for them as she watched their slow, arthritic gait up and down the alleys. Most of them were white horses, a dirty white as if their original colors had turned white with age, like the hair on an old man's head. They had enormous hooves with iron shoes that clacked down the alleys over the broken glass, which squealed against the concrete when the rusty, metal-rimmed wheels of the wagon ground over it. Their muzzles were pink without hair, and their tongues lolled out gray; their teeth were huge and yellow. Over their eyes were black blinders, around their shoulders a heavy black harness that looked always ready to slip off, leather straps hung all about their bodies. They ate from black, worn leather sacks tied over their faces, and as they ate, the flies flew up from their droppings and climbed all over their thick bodies and the horses swished at them with stringy tails.

The Ragmen drove down the crooked, interconnecting alleys crying, "Rags ol irn, rags ol irn," and the boys waited for a wagon to pass, hiding behind fences or garbage cans; and as soon as it passed they would follow, running half bent over so that they couldn't be seen if the Ragman turned around over the piles heaped on his wagon. They would run to the tailgate and grab on to it, swinging up, the taller ones, like John, stretching their legs onto the rear axle, the shorter ones just hanging as the wagon rolled along. Sometimes one of the bolder boys would try to climb up on the wagon itself and throw off some of the junk. The Ragman would see him and pull the reins, stopping the wagon. He would begin gesturing and yelling at the boys, who jumped from the wagon and stood back laughing and hollering, "Rags ol irn, rags ol irn!" Sometimes he'd grab a makeshift whip, a piece of clothesline tied to a stick, and stagger after them as they scattered laughing before him, disappearing over fences and down gangways only to reappear again around the corner of some other alley; or, lying flattened on a garage roof, they'd suddenly jump up and shower the wagon with garbage as it passed beneath.

Mary could never fully understand why her brother participated. He wasn't a bully like Leon Sisca and certainly not cruel like Denny Zmiga, who tortured cats. She sensed the boys vaguely condemned the Ragmen for the sad condition of their horses. But that was only a small part of it, for often the horses as well as their masters were harassed. She thought it was a venial sin and wondered if John confessed it the Thursday before each First Friday, when they would go together to confession in the afternoon: Bless me Father for I have sinned, I threw garbage on a Ragman five times this month. For your penance say five Our Fathers and five Hail Marys, go in peace. She never mentioned this to him, feeling that whatever made him do it was a part of what made him generally unafraid, a part of what the boys felt when they elected him captain of the St. Roman Grammar School baseball team. She couldn't bear it if he thought she was a dumb girl. She never snitched on him. If she approached him when he was surrounded by his friends, he would loudly announce, "All right, nobody swear while Mary's here."

At home he often took her into his confidence. This was what she liked the most, when, after supper, while her parents watched TV in the parlor, he would come into her room, where she was doing her homework, and lie down on her bed and start talking, telling her who among his friends was a good first sacker, or which one of the girls in his class tried to get him to dance with her at the school party, just talking and sometimes even asking her opinion on something like if she thought he should let his hair grow long like that idiot Peter Noskin, who couldn't even make the team as a right fielder. What did she think of guys like that? She tried to tell him things back. How Sister Mary Valentine had caught Leon Sisca in the girls' washroom yesterday. And then one night he told her about Raymond Cruz, which she knew was a secret because their father had warned John not to hang around with him even if he was the best pitcher on the team. He told her how after school he and Raymond Cruz had followed a Ragman to Hobotown, which was far away, past Western Avenue, on the other side of the river, down by the river and the railroad tracks, and that they had a regular town there without any streets. They lived among huge heaps of junk, rubbled lots tangled with smashed, rusting cars and bathtubs, rotting mounds of rags and paper, woodpiles infested with river rats. Their wagons were all lined up and the horses kept in a deserted factory with broken windows. They lived in shacks that were falling apart, some of them made out of old boxcars, and there was a blacksmith with a burning forge working in a ruined shed made of bricks and timbers with a roof of canvas.

He told her how they had snuck around down the riverbank in the high weeds and watched the Ragmen come in from all parts of the city, pulled by their tired horses, hundreds of Ragmen arriving in silence, and how they assembled in front of a great fire burning in the middle of all the shacks, where something was cooking in a huge, charred pot.

Their scroungy dogs scratched and circled around the fire while the Ragmen stood about and seemed to be trading among one another: bales of worn clothing for baskets of tomatoes, bushels of fruit for twisted metals, cases of dust-filled bottles for scorched couches and lamps with frazzled wires. They knelt, peering out of the weeds and watching them, and then Ray whispered let's sneak around to the building where the horses are kept and look at them.

So they crouched through the weeds and ran from shack to shack until they came to the back of the old factory. They could smell the horses and hay inside and hear the horses sneezing. They snuck in through a busted window. The factory was dark and full of spiderwebs, and they felt their way through a passage that entered into a high-ceilinged hall where the horses were stabled. It was dim; rays of sun sifted down through the dust from the broken roof. The horses didn't look the same in the dimness without their harnesses. They looked huge and beautiful, and when you reached to pat them, their muscles quivered so that you flinched with fright.

"Wait'll the guys hear about this," John said.

And Ray whispered, "Let's steal one! We can take him to the river and ride him."

John didn't know what to say. Ray was fourteen. His parents were divorced. He had failed a year in school and often hung around with high-school guys. Everybody knew that he had been caught in a stolen car but that the police let him go because he was so much younger than the other guys. He was part Mexican and knew a lot about horses. John didn't like the idea of stealing.

"We couldn't get one out of here," he said.

"Sure we could," Ray said. "We could get on one and gallop out with him before they knew what was going on."

"Suppose we get caught," John said.

"Who'd believe the Ragmen anyway?" Ray asked him. "They can't even speak English. You chicken?"

So they picked out a huge white horse to ride, who stood still and uninterested when John boosted Ray up on his back and then Ray reached down and pulled him up. Ray held his mane and John held on to Ray's waist. Ray nudged his heels into the horse's flanks and he began to move, slowly swaying toward the light of the doorway.

"As soon as we get outside," Ray whispered, "hold on. I'm gonna goose him."

John's palms were sweating by this time because being on this horse felt like straddling a blimp as it rose over the roofs. When they got to the door, Ray hollered, "Heya!" and kicked his heels hard, and the horse bolted out, and before he knew what had happened, John felt himself sliding, dropping a long way, and then felt the sudden hard smack of the hay-strewn floor. He looked up and realized he had never made it out of the barn, and then he heard the shouting and barking of the dogs and, looking out, saw Ray half riding, half hanging from the horse, which reared again and again, surrounded by the shouting Ragmen, and he saw the look on Ray's face as he was bucked from the horse into their arms. There was a paralyzed second when they all glanced toward him standing in the doorway of the barn, and then he whirled around and stumbled past the now-pitching bulks of horses whinnying all about him and found the passage, struggling through it, bumping into walls, spiderwebs sticking to his face, with the shouts and barks gaining on him, and then he was out the window and running up a hill of weeds, crushed coal slipping under his feet, skidding up and down two more hills, down railroad tracks, not turning around, just running until he could no longer breathe, and above him he saw a bridge and clawed up the grassy embankment till he reached it.

It was rush hour and the bridge was crowded with people going home, factory workers carrying lunch pails and businessmen with attaché cases. The street was packed with traffic, and he didn't know where he was or what he should do about Ray. He decided to go home and see what would happen. He'd call Ray that night, and if he wasn't home, then he'd tell them about the Ragmen. But he couldn't find his way back. Finally he had to ask a cop where he was, and the cop put him on a trolley car that got him home.

He called Ray about eight o'clock, and his mother answered the phone and told him Ray had just got in and went right to bed, and John asked her if he could speak to him, and she said she'd go see, and he heard her set down the receiver and her footsteps walk away. He realized his own heartbeat was no longer deafening and felt the knots in his stomach loosen. Then he heard Ray's mother say that she was sorry but that Ray didn't want to talk to him.

The next day, at school, he saw Ray and asked him what happened, if he was angry that he had run out on him, and Ray said, no, nothing happened, to forget it. He kept asking Ray how he got away, but Ray wouldn't say anything until John mentioned telling the other guys about it. Ray said if he told anybody he'd deny it ever happened, that there was such a place. John thought he was just kidding, but when he told the guys, Ray told them John made the whole thing up, and they almost got into a fight, pushing each other back and forth, nobody taking the first swing, until the guys stepped between them and broke it up. John lost his temper and said he'd take any of the guys who wanted to go next Saturday to see for themselves. They could go on their bikes and hide them in the weeds by the river and sneak up on the Ragmen. Ray said go on.

So on Saturday John and six guys met at his place and peddled toward the river and railroad tracks, down the busy trucking streets, where the semis passed you so fast your bike seemed about to be sucked away by the draft. They got to Western Avenue and the river, and it looked the same and didn't look the same. They left the street and pumped their bikes down a dirt road left through the weeds by bulldozers, passing rusty barges moored to the banks, seemingly abandoned in the oily river. They passed a shack or two, but they were empty. John kept looking for the three mounds of black cinders as a landmark but couldn't find them. They rode their bikes down the railroad tracks, and it wasn't like being in the center of the city at all, with the smell of milkweeds and the noise of birds and crickets all about them and the spring sun glinting down the railroad tracks. No one was around. It was like being far out in the country. They rode until they could see the skyline of downtown, skyscrapers rising up through the smoke of chimneys like a horizon of jagged mountains in the mist. By now everyone was kidding him about the Ragmen, and finally he had to admit he couldn't find them, and they gave up. They all peddled back, kidding him, and he bought everybody Cokes, and they admitted they had had a pretty good time anyway, even though he sure as hell was some storyteller.

And he figured something must have happened to Ray. It hit him Sunday night, lying in bed trying to sleep, and he knew he'd have to talk to him about it Monday when he saw him at school, but on Monday Ray was absent and was absent on Tuesday, and on Wednesday they found out that Ray had run away from home and no one could find him.

❖

No one ever found him, and he wasn't there in June when John and his classmates filed down the aisle, their maroon robes flowing and white tassels swinging almost in time to the organ, to receive their diplomas and shake hands with Father Mike. And the next week it was summer, and she was permitted to go to the beach with her girlfriends. Her girlfriends came over and giggled whenever John came into the room.

On Sundays they went to late mass. She wore her flowered-print dress and a white mantilla in church when she sat beside John among the adults. After mass they'd stop at the corner of Twenty-fifth Street on their way home and buy *palatski* and walk home eating it with its crispness melting and the sweet honey crust becoming chewy. She remembered how she used to pretend it was manna they'd been rewarded with for keeping the Sabbath. It tasted extra good because she had skipped breakfast. She fasted before receiving Communion.

Then it began to darken earlier, and the kids played tag and rolivio in the dusk and hid from each other behind trees and in doorways, and the girls laughed and blushed when the boys chased and tagged them. She had her own secret hiding place down the block, in a garden under a lilac bush, where no one could find her; and she would lie there listening to her name called in the darkness, Mary Mary free free free, by so many voices.

She shopped downtown with her mother at night for new school clothes, skirts, not dresses, green ribbons for her dark hair, and shoes without buckles, like slippers a ballerina wears. And that night she tried them on for John, dancing in her nightgown, and he said you're growing up. And later her mother came into her room—only the little bed lamp was burning—and explained to her what growing up was like. And after her mother left, she picked up a little rag doll that was kept as an ornament on her dresser and tried to imagine having a child, really having a child, it coming out of her body, and she looked at herself in the mirror and stood close to it and looked at the colors of her eyes: brown around the edges and then turning a milky gray that seemed to be smoking behind crystal and toward the center the gray turning green, getting greener till it was almost violet near her pupils. And in the black mirror of her pupils she saw herself looking at herself.

The next day, school started again and she was a sixth-grader. John was in high school, and Leon Sisca, who had grown much bigger over the summer and smoked, sneered at her and said, "Who'll protect you now?" She made a visit to the church at lunchtime and dropped a dime in the metal box by the ruby vigil lights and lit a candle high up on the rack with a long wax wick and said a prayer to the Blessed Virgin.

And it was late in October, and leaves wafted from the catalpa trees on their way to church on Sunday and fell like withered fans into the birdbaths, turning the water brown. They were walking back from mass, and she was thinking how little she saw John anymore, how he no longer came to her room to talk, and she said, "Let's do something together."

"What?" he asked.

"Let's follow the Palatski Man."

"Why would you want to do that?"

"I don't know," she said. "We could find out where he lives, where he makes his stuff. He won't come around pretty soon. Maybe we could go to his house in the winter and buy things from him."

John looked at her. Her hair, like his, was blowing about in the wind. "All right," he said.

So they waited at a corner where a man was raking leaves into a pile to burn, but each time he built the pile and turned to scrape a few more leaves from his small lawn, the wind blew and the leaves whirled off from the pile and sprayed out as if alive over their heads, and then the wind suddenly died, and they floated back about the raking man into the grass softly, looking like wrinkled snow. And in a rush of leaves they closed their eyes against, the Palatski Man pushed by.

They let him go down the block. He wasn't hard to follow, he went so slow, stopping at corners for customers. They didn't have to sneak behind him because he never turned around. They followed him down the streets, and one street became another until they were out of their neighborhood, and the clothes the people wore became poorer and brighter. They went through the next parish, and there was less stopping because it was a poorer parish where more Mexicans lived, and the children yelled in Spanish, and they felt odd in their new Sunday clothes.

"Let's go back," John said.

But Mary thought there was something in his voice that wasn't sure, and she took his arm and mock-pleaded, "No-o-o-o, this is fun, let's see where he goes."

The Palatski Man went up the streets, past the trucking lots full of semis without cabs, where the wind blew more grit and dirty papers than leaves, where he stopped hardly at all. Then past blocks of mesh-windowed factories shut down for Sunday and the streets empty and the pavements powdered with brown glass from broken beer bottles. They walked hand in hand a block behind the white, bent figure of the Palatski Man pushing his cart over the fissured sidewalk. When he crossed streets and looked from side to side for traffic, they jumped into doorways, afraid he might turn around.

He crossed Western Avenue, which was a big street and so looked emptier than any of the others without traffic on it. They followed him down Western Avenue and over the rivet-studded, aluminum-girdered bridge that spanned the river, watching the pigeons flitting through the cables. Just past the bridge he turned into a pitted asphalt road that trucks used for hauling their cargoes to freight trains. It wound into the acres of endless lots and railroad yards behind the factories along the river.

John stopped. "We can't go any further," he said.

"Why?" she asked. "It's getting interesting."

"I've been here before," he said.

"When?"

"I don't remember, but I feel like I've been here before."

"C'mon, silly," she said, and tugged his arm with all her might and opened her eyes very wide, and John let himself be tugged along, and they both started laughing. But by now the Palatski Man had disappeared around a curve in the road, and they had to run to catch up. When they turned the bend, they just caught sight of him going over a hill, and the asphalt road they had to run up had turned to cinder. At the top of the hill Mary cried, "Look!" and pointed off to the left, along the river. They saw a wheat field in the center of the city, with the wheat blowing and waving, and the Palatski Man, half man and half willowy grain, was pushing his cart through the field past a scarecrow with straw arms outstretched and huge black crows perched on them.

"It looks like he's hanging on a cross," Mary said.

"Let's go," John said, and she thought he meant turn back home and was ready to agree because his voice sounded so determined, but he moved forward instead to follow the Palatski Man.

"Where can he be going?" Mary said.

But John just looked at her and put his finger to his lips. They followed single file down a trail trod smooth and twisting through the wheat field. When they passed the scarecrow, the crows flapped off in great iridescent flutters, cawing at them while the scarecrow hung as if guarding a field of wings. Then, at the edge of the field, the cinder path resumed sloping downhill toward the river.

John pointed and said, "The mounds of coal."

And she saw three black mounds rising up in the distance and sparkling in the sun.

"C'mon," John said, "we have to get off the path."

He led her down the slope and into the weeds that blended with the river grasses, rushes, and cattails. They sneaked through the weeds, which pulled at her dress and scratched her legs. John led the way; he seemed to know where he was going. He got down on his hands and knees and motioned for her to do the same, and they crawled forward without making a sound. Then John lay flat on his stomach, and she crawled beside him and flattened out. He parted the weeds, and she looked out and saw a group of men standing around a kettle on a fire and dressed in a strange assortment of ill-fitting suits, either too small or too large and baggy. None of the suit pieces matched, trousers blue and the suitcoat brown, striped pants and checked coats, countless combinations of colors. They wore crushed hats of all varieties: bowlers, straws, stetsons, derbies, homburgs. Their ties were the strangest of all, misshapen and dangling to their knees in wild designs of flowers, swirls, and polka dots.

"Who are they?" she whispered.

"The Ragmen. They must be dressed for Sunday," John hissed.

And then she noticed the shacks behind the men, with the empty wagons parked in front and the stacks of junk from uprooted basements and strewn attics, even the gutted factory just the way John had described it. She saw the dogs suddenly jump up barking and whining, and all the men by the fire turn around as the Palatski Man wheeled his cart into their midst.

He gestured to them, and they all parted as he walked to the fire, where he stood staring into the huge black pot. He turned and said something to one of them, and the man began to stir whatever was in the pot, and then the Palatski Man dipped a small ladle into it and raised it up, letting its contents pour back into the pot, and Mary felt herself get dizzy and gasp as she saw the bright red fluid in the sun and heard John exclaim, "Blood!" And she didn't want to see any more, how the men came to the pot and dipped their fingers in it and licked them off, nodding and smiling. She saw the horses filing out of their barn, looking ponderous and naked without their harnesses. She hid her face in her arms and wouldn't look, and then she heard the slow, sorrowful chanting and off-key wheezing behind it. And she looked up and realized all the Ragmen, like a choir of bums, had removed their crushed hats and stood bareheaded in the wind, singing. Among them someone worked a dilapidated accordion, squeezing out a mournful, foreign melody. In the center stood the Palatski Man, leading them with his arms like a conductor and sometimes intoning a word that all would echo in a chant. Their songs rose and fell but always rose again, sometimes nasal, then shifting into a rich baritone, building always louder and louder, more sorrowful, until the Palatski Man rang his bell and suddenly everything was silent. Not men or dogs or accordion or birds or crickets or wind made a sound. Only her breathing and a far-off throb that she seemed to feel more than hear, as if all the church bells in the city were tolling an hour. The sun was in the center of the sky. Directly below it stood the Palatski Man raising a *palatski.*

The Ragmen had all knelt. They rose and started a procession leading to where she and John hid in the grass. Then John was up and yelling, "Run!" and she scrambled to her feet, John dragging her by the arm. She tried to run but her legs wouldn't obey her. They felt so rubbery pumping through the weeds and John pulling her faster than she could go with the weeds tripping her and the vines clutching like fingers around her ankles.

Ragmen rose up in front of them and they stopped and ran the other way but Ragmen were there too. Ragmen were everywhere in an embracing circle, so they stopped and stood still, holding hands.

"Don't be afraid," John told her.

And she wasn't. Her legs wouldn't move and she didn't care. She just didn't want to run anymore, choking at the acrid smell of the polluted river. Through her numbness she heard John's small voice lost over and over in the open daylight repeating, "We weren't doin' anything."

The Ragmen took them back to where the Palatski Man stood before the fire and the bubbling pot. John started to say something but stopped when the Palatski Man raised his finger to his lips. One of the Ragmen brought a bushel of shiny apples and another a handful of pointed little sticks. The Palatski Man took an apple and inserted the stick and dipped it into the pot and took it out coated with red. The red crystallized and turned hard, and suddenly she realized it was a red candy apple that he was handing her. She took it from his hand and held it dumbly while he made another for John and a third for himself. He bit into his and motioned for them to do the same. She looked up at John standing beside her, flushed and sweaty, and she bit into her apple. It was sweeter than anything she'd ever tasted, with the red candy crunching in her mouth, melting, mingling with apple juice.

And then from his cart he took a giant *palatski*, ten times bigger than any she had ever seen, and broke it again and again, handing the tiny bits to the circle of Ragmen, where they were passed from mouth to mouth. When there was only a small piece left, he broke it three ways and offered one to John. She saw it disappear in John's hand and watched him raise his hand to his mouth and at the same time felt him squeeze her hand very hard. The Palatski Man handed her a part. Honey stretched into threads from its torn edges. She put it in her mouth, expecting the crisp wafer and honey taste, but it was so bitter it brought tears to her eyes. She fought them back and swallowed, trying not to screw up her face, not knowing whether he had tricked her or given her a gift she didn't understand. He spoke quietly to one of the Ragmen in a language she couldn't follow and pointed to an enormous pile of rags beside a nearby shack. The man trudged to the pile and began sorting through it and returned with a white ribbon of immaculate, shining silk. The Palatski Man gave it to her, then turned and walked away, disappearing into the shack. As soon as he was gone, the circle of Ragmen broke and they trudged away, leaving the children standing dazed before the fire.

"Let's get out of here," John said. They turned and began walking slowly, afraid the Ragmen would regroup at any second, but no one paid any attention to them. They walked away. Back through the wheat field, past silently perched crows, over the hill, down the cinder path that curved and became the pitted asphalt road. They walked over the Western Avenue bridge, which shook as a green trolley, empty with Sunday, clattered across it. They stopped in the middle of the bridge, and John opened his hand, and she saw the piece of *palatski* crushed into a little sour ball, dirty and pasty with sweat.

"Did you eat yours?" he asked.

"Yes," she said.

"I tried to stop you," he said. "Didn't you feel me squeezing your hand? It might have been poisoned."

"No," she lied, so he wouldn't worry, "it tasted fine."

"Nobody believed me," John said.

"I believed you."

"They'll see now."

And then he gently took the ribbon that she still unconsciously held in her hand—she had an impulse to clench her fist but didn't—and before she could say anything, he threw it over the railing into the river. They watched it, caught in the drafts of wind under the bridge, dipping and gliding among the wheeling pigeons, finally touching the green water and floating away.

"You don't want the folks to see that," John said. "They'd get all excited and nothing happened. I mean nothing really happened, we're both all right."

"Yes," she said. They looked at each other. Sunlight flashing through latticed girders made them squint; it reflected from the slits of eyes and off the river when their gaze dropped. Wind swooped over the railing and tangled their hair.

"You're the best girl I ever knew," John told her.

They both began to laugh, so hard they almost cried, and John stammered out, "We're late for dinner—I bet we're gonna really get it," and they hurried home.

They were sent to bed early that night without being permitted to watch TV. She undressed and put on her nightgown and climbed under her covers, feeling the sad, hollow Sunday-night feeling when the next morning will be Monday and the weekend is dying. The feeling always reminded her of all the past Sunday nights she'd had it, and she thought of all the future Sunday nights when it would come again. She wished John could come into her room so they could talk. She lay in bed tossing and seeking the cool places under her pillow with her arms and in the nooks of her blanket with her toes. She listened to the whole house go to sleep: the TV shut off after the late news, the voices of her parents discussing whether the doors had been locked for the night. She felt herself drifting to sleep and tried to think her nightly prayer, the Hail Mary before she slept, but it turned into a half dream that she woke out of with a faint recollection of Gabriel's wings, and she lay staring at the familiar shapes of furniture in her dark room. She heard the wind outside like a low whinny answered by cats. At last she climbed out of her bed and looked out the lace-curtained window. Across her backyard, over the catalpa tree, the moon hung low in the cold sky. It looked like a giant *palatski* snagged in the twigs. And then she heard the faint tinkle of the bell.

He stood below, staring up, the moon, like silver eyeballs, shining in the centers of his dark glasses. His horse, a windy white stallion, stamped and snorted behind him, and a gust of leaves funneled along the ground and swirled through the streetlight, and some of them stuck in the horse's tangled mane while its hooves kicked sparks in the dark alley. He offered her a *palatski*.

She ran from the window to the mirror and looked at herself in the dark, feeling her teeth growing and hair pushing through her skin in the tender parts of her body that had been bare and her breasts swelling like apples from her flat chest and her blood burning, and then in a lapse of wind, when the leaves fell back to earth, she heard his gold bell jangle again as if silver and knew that it was time to go.

The Cat Woman

There was an old *buzka* on Luther Street known as the Cat Woman, not because she kept cats but because she disposed of the neighborhood's excess kittens. Fathers would bring them in cardboard boxes at night after the children were asleep and she would drown them in her wash machine. The wash machine was in the basement, an ancient model with a galvanized-metal tub that stood on legs and had a wringer. A thick cord connected it to a socket that hung from the ceiling and when she turned it on the light bulb in the basement would flicker and water begin to pour.

She lived with her crazy grandson, Swantek. His first name was George, but everyone, including the nuns at school, called him Swantek. It could be spit out like a swear word. Even his *buzka* called him that, after his father, Big Swantek, a brawling drunk who'd beat her daughter regularly, then disappeared after she died. It was rumored Swantek's mother had committed suicide and that's why her funeral was held in a Russian Orthodox parish across the city.

One day Swantek took clothespins and hung the bodies of the drowned kittens by their tails from the clothesline in the backyard—like a line of wet socks covered with lint. When the Cat Woman saw it, she chased him around the yard and out the alley gate, beating his legs with a broomstick. Mrs. Panova, the old lady in the house next door, went inside as if nothing unusual were happening. But the people in the big apartment building across the alley hung out of their windows cheering and laughing like an audience in a gallery.

Despite the black-and-blue marks that appeared again and again on his body, it seemed that as the Cat Woman got older, Swantek got crazier. He sneaked around the railroad tracks instead of going to school. He took to sleeping nights in the abandoned cars along the dead-end side streets behind Spiegel's warehouse. When winter came the cops chased him out. The next night, every junk car down the block went up in flames.

That winter he was seen crouching naked by the chimney on the peak of his roof, beckoning to ten-year-old stick-legged Bonnie Buford as she trudged down the alley to school. Finally, his grandma seemed to give up on him and the bodies began to accumulate on the clothesline. People believed that Swantek had even run a few through the wringer and after a while nobody brought boxes of litters anymore.

Within a year the neighborhood was full of stray cats. Toms sprayed fences, sides of houses, inside hallways and sheds, so that after a rain it seemed the entire world reeked of cat sexuality.

When summer came with its sweltering nights, insomnia spread like a plague. Windows were raised in the huge apartment buildings, and after dark the long alleyways amplified screeching operas of cats. Curses and garbage rained down from the fire escapes. One night in August someone opened up with a .22.

By then irritability had become a habit. In the dime store, under slowly revolving ceiling fans, women argued over places in line and babies bawled. Gangs of older boys carrying baseball bats and knives patrolled heat-vapored streets. Behind sun-beaten shades bodies in sweat-stained underwear tossed in fitful naps.

Taverns filled. Nights grew frenzied with boozy shouting and jukebox music. News of those nights spread and people swarmed from other parts of the city to release their own madness where it couldn't threaten their everyday lives. Men drank and tried to sleep with other men's wives. Windows shook as sirens shrieked by. Even the soundest sleepers, who'd slept through the cats, were kept awake, pacing their rooms. At dawn strangers stumbled about sidewalks spattered with vomit and blood, trying to remember where they'd parked their cars.

Neighborhood men lost their jobs and stood on corners watching traffic, sipping wine from twisted paper bags. Buildings turned shabby. People rolled their car windows up when they had to ride through, staring out at dirty sidewalks, at shivering bums, faded women, ragged kids, cats blinking from doorways.

No one brought laundry anymore to the old woman who had supported herself and her grandson by taking in wash. Her basement and yard still smelled of powdered soap, but everywhere the clothes were gray. She'd long ago stopped flinging bread crusts onto the garage roof for sparrows. Every other day, the Russian lady next door invited her in for cabbage soup. She'd take a bowl back to her grandson, carefully wash the dish, bring it back two days later saying, "*Spaceeba*, missus, for the soup and your bowl."

And Mrs. Panova would tell her, "Come in and have another. I always have a pot on the stove."

The two ladies sat at the table, spoons clacking against the sides of the bowl, blowing on each spoonful with nothing more to say, radio on the polka station. And later, at home, the Cat Woman fit her cardboard-soled house slippers over her bandaged, swollen feet and crept through her house, fingering the rosary.

But Swantek needed more than soup and prayers. He'd moved into the basement, never coming out, sleeping on a pile of old drapes beside the empty furnace, vomiting up cabbage in the corners and covering it with newspapers, touching himself in the dark and smelling an aching smell like bleach, hearing cats yowl on the other side of the snowdrifted black-paned windows, the floorboards creaking continually overhead, where his *buzka*, the Cat Woman, padded.

Blood Soup

Busha was calling him.

He ran into her room. She lay in the dark clutching the crucifix, her toothless gums chewing with prayer.

"Oh, Busha," he said, "nobody's home."

She closed her eyes and her crouplike breath came easier.

"*Usiądź*," she whispered, patting the bed for him to sit.

He sat beside her for the first time since they'd brought her back half conscious from the hospital. It was only a matter of time, they'd been told. But she'd hung on for two weeks.

"You take care of me now, Stefush." She smiled. "Remember how I take care of you?" Her arm rose to smooth his hair back, skin transparent as a lampshade, bones like yellow candles beneath the network of veins.

"How are you feeling, Busha? Can I get you something?"

"Dying, Stefush."

"No, you're not, Busha. You're going to get well."

"Too old. No strength." She held his wrist and closed her eyes again. He was suddenly afraid that she would die with only him there. The room seemed oppressive, reeking of camphor and Vick's, shades drawn against the sunlight, the tops of the nightstands and bureaus cluttered with medicine bottles and photographs of all her children and grandchildren. Even now Busha made him feel that secret he'd always felt between them, that in her seemingly unlimited power to love them all she loved him specially. It was the kind of love he thought must have come from the Old Country—instinctive, unquestioning—like her strength, something foreign that he couldn't find in himself, that hadn't even been transmitted to his mother or any of Busha's other children.

The holy pictures of Jesus and Mary gazed down from over Busha's bed with sorrowful eyes, hair flowing, their flaming hearts crowned with thorns, pierced by swords, and dripping blood. When he was little, Busha would give him a dime if he kissed them and he could still remember the taste of dusty glass on his lips. He wished he believed in them strongly enough now to pray for her. She was sweating.

"Can I get you water?"

She opened her eyes. "*Zupa*"—she swallowed—"soup."

"What kind, Busha? Chicken noodle? Tomato? I'll make some."

She rolled her head *no* on the pillow, making a sour face, smacking her gray tongue. "*Czarnina.*"

"What?"

"*Czarnina*. Blood soup. *Rozumiesz?*" she asked.

"Yes," he answered, he understood. He remembered her making it years ago, a strong-smelling mixture of carrots, apples, prunes, flour, sour cream, parsley, thyme, and duck's blood. She'd kept two full pickle jars of the blood in the refrigerator and he would open it late at night to stare at them, liverish red beside the sweating-glass gallon of milk, waxed paper rubber-banded over their tops, and featherless duck heads on the lower shelf floating in a pot of clear water. It was Easter, rainy, they were all at Busha's, arriving with colored hard-boiled eggs, ham, kraut, *kielbasa,* freshly grated horseradish. When his uncles saw the soup simmering on the stove they began laughing and joking.

"Hey, Ma must have been feeling run-down again."

"Time for the family's oral transfusion."

They sat at the Ping-Pong table on the back porch as she ladled it steaming into bowls.

"Try, Stefush, Make you strong. Grandpa loved it."

But he wouldn't.

"It's fruit soup, Stefush. Just take a taste."

He sipped off the tip of a spoon. Heavy and sweetish, the taste coating his tongue like velvet, but beneath the sweetness something dark and overly rich, like marrow. No, he insisted, he didn't want any more. He was ready to cry.

"Take jar from dresser and go to Józef's," Busha said, pulling herself up from the pillow, squeezing his wrist. "He give you."

"That's your holy water in there, Busha." He didn't try to explain that his uncle Józef had sold the meat market he'd owned the last twenty years.

"Bring me."

He brought her the Miracle Whip jar. The evaporating holy water looked like urine with a cloud of residue at the bottom. She dipped her fingers and made the sign of the cross, then spilled the rest onto the wilting lily someone had propped beside the bedpan.

"You get for me, Stefush." Again it was like a secret between them, a magic to keep her alive.

"Okay," he promised. His legs were weak, his back

sweaty. All he wanted was to get out of that room. His parents would be back soon anyway.

"Take quarter for yourself," she said, pointing to the little change purse on the dresser.

"No, Busha, you don't have to give me money. I'm too old."

"Stevie, take quarter. I know you smoke."

He unsnapped the purse and took a quarter. "Thanks," he said.

He washed the jar out with hot water and put it in a bag, then took two dollars from the teapot where his mother kept loose change. His brother, Dove, was in the backyard throwing a rubber ball off the brick wall of the apartment building next door. In the sunlight, with traffic passing, it hardly seemed real to Steve that he'd just been in a dark room with a dying woman.

"Wanta come with?" Steve asked.

"Where to?"

"Uncle Joe's old meat market."

"Taking the Alley Heartaches?"

"Yeah."

Dove had nicknamed them Alley Heartaches earlier that summer when they walked the alleys instead of streets to the dentist. The alleys made them almost forget where they were going. Trees arched over wooden backyard fences like a green arcade, the fences were lined with garbage cans to pick through, smells blasted from black ventilators behind stores and factories. Steve had made up a double called the Butchie, who lived in the Alley Heartaches, distinguishable from Steve only because of the clothespin he wore in his hair. The Butchie would ambush them whenever Steve ran ahead and turned into a gangway. Dove would find Steve unconscious, a victim of the Butchie, or the Butchie himself would appear, grinning like a maniac beneath his clothespin, to bombard Dove with garbage. But Steve didn't feel like the Butchie now. They walked along in silence. He hadn't even bothered bringing a clothespin.

"I thought you were suppose to watch Busha," Dove said.

"Busha *told* me to go."

"For what?"

"*Zupa.*"

"*Zupa?*"

"Soup, jerk. We're going to get Busha soup."

"Why does she want soup?"

Steve ignored him. Instead he started humming, then singing:

> "Gimme dat *zupa zupa zupa.*
> Gimme dat oompha oompha oompha."

He sang it over and over in different voices, making a sound like a tuba at the end.

"They're gonna be mad when they get home if you're not there," Dove said.

"Shut up and sing, dimp. And march!"

> "Gimme dat *zupa zupa zupa.*
> Gimme dat oompha oompha oompha."

The sign on the window still read JOE'S MEATS. Plucked chickens dangled scaly yellow claws above the faded plastic parsley and spattered sheets of butcher paper. Steve looked for the skinned rabbits his uncle usually hung among the chickens but there weren't any.

Inside, shoppers crowded before the glass meat counters while the butchers called out numbers. A lot of the talk was in Spanish. Little Mexican kids played in the sawdust on the floor, sweeping it into mounds as if they were at the beach, the way Steve remembered doing when he was smaller. He and Dove stood at the end of the counter watching the butchers in their red-smeared aprons lugging sides of meat and trays heaped with innards from the clunking, safelike freezer door.

Big Antek was still there, behind his wooden chopping block, surrounded by huge knives, hacksaws, and cleavers, his boozer's nose like a clown's, whacking the cleaver through gristle with the same abandon that had cost him three of the fingers on his left hand. He saw them and grinned. When he came over he had a cold hotdog for each.

"What you guys want?"

Steve slipped the empty Miracle Whip jar out of the bag. "My grandma needs duck's blood to make soup."

"We don't sell fresh blood no more," Antek said. "It's against health regulations."

"You mean nobody can get it anymore?"

"I can get Busha some," Antek whispered, "but not till Saturday. We only get ducks for the weekend now. How's she doing?"

"Bad. Everyone's waiting for her to die."

"I know a guy you can get some from right away, maybe," Antek said. "At least he used to have it. Ain't seen him since around Christmas. We used to drink together when I worked at the Yards. He's a little crazy. Raises pigeons. Sometimes sleeps on the roof with them. In fact, that's what they call him—Pan Gowumpe—'Mr. Pigeon' in English." Antek had scribbled the name and an address on a torn corner of butcher paper. "Be careful in that neighborhood," he cautioned, dropping his voice, "the coloreds are moving in."

They left the meat market, Dove puffing at his hotdog and flicking it as if it were a big cigar. On the next corner, by Goldblatt's, the blind man played accordion. He played with his back to Twenty-sixth Street and the music had always seemed like an invisible boundary to Steve.

"Here, give him this quarter and watch his dog," he told Dove.

The dog raised its wolfish head off his paws and opened its eyes when the coin clunked into the cup. The eyes gleamed silverish blue-green, like mother-of-pearl.

"See? The dog's blind too."

They crossed the boundary of wheezing music. A block down, a loudspeaker over the door of a used-furniture store crackled old Temptations hits. The sidewalk was jammed with secondhand furniture and refrigerators. Instead of supermarkets and department stores the street was lined with Goodwill clothing shops, noisy bars, and abandoned storefronts.

"Let's go in here and look around," Dove said before an Army-surplus store.

"We don't have time to fool around. Busha's waiting. And don't stare at people," Steve said as a bearded black man went by, testifying to the traffic.

Steve kept checking addresses against the paper Antek had given them. Finally, they stopped before a maroon-brick apartment building surrounded by a broken pipe fence. Doorbells dangled from frayed, disconnected wires in the entrance hall. The cracked plaster beneath the mailboxes was crayoned with names from years of tenants.

"This place doesn't even have an address," Dove said.

"Well, this is where it *should* be. Here's Gowumpe—fourth floor."

The bulbs were burned out on the stairway. They climbed toward the foggy gleam of the skylight. At the far end of the hallway on four, the fire-escape exit stood ajar, emitting a streak of blue summer sky, though hardly enough light to see the doors.

"Now what?" Dove asked.

"It didn't give an apartment number."

They could hear radios playing behind some of the doors.

"Pan Gowumpe! *Pan Gowumpe!*" Dove hollered down the corridor.

"Shut up! Jesus Christ! You want the crazy people to come out?"

They ducked through the exit and crouched on the fire-escape landing, but none of the doors opened.

"Let's try the roof," Steve said. He only half meant it. A narrow metal ladder ran up the side of the building and over the roof.

"I'm not climbing that," Dove said.

"Okay, chickenshit, then wait here and hold the bottle."

"I'm not waiting here alone."

"Then climb the goddamn ladder."

The rungs were rusty and when Steve got on behind Dove the bolts moved in the crumbling mortar and for a moment it seemed as if the entire four-story fire escape were swaying loose against the side of the building.

"Yaaahhh," Dove screamed.

"Keep moving or you'll get paralyzed," Steve said.

Dove kept climbing slowly, hand over hand. Once over the edge, he sat down hard on the roof, digging his fingernails into the tar as if the building might suddenly tilt and slide him off.

A wind that hadn't been blowing on the street fanned across the blazing tar. It was tacky beneath their gym shoes. A twisted TV antenna lay embedded on its side, tangled in wire. A wooden shed the size of a newspaper stand leaned by the chimney. Beyond it, against the peaked skylight, a row of coops stood on a raised wooden platform. Hard corn scattered below them like gravel. The panes of the skylight were crusted with pigeon droppings and splashes of whitewash.

They walked over to the coops. Two pigeons fluttered off. They watched them sail away over the roofs and trees, and circle the copper green steeple of St. Kasimir's.

"I wonder where all the other pigeons are," Steve said.

A cooing howl, half pigeon, half ghost, came from behind them. They froze.

"Go away 'fore you get pushed off," a voice rasped from the wooden shed.

"We're looking for Mr. Gowumpe. Antek from Joe's meat market gave us his address," Steve said quickly.

"I know you made the massacre! I can identify you!"

The wooden door opened a crack. A weasel-shaped face peered out with whitish eyes.

"All we came for was to buy some duck's blood for soup for my sick grandma. See?" Steve held up the Miracle Whip jar.

"How much you pay?"

"Are you Pan Gowumpe?"

The door opened out wider. A small, stooped black man wearing a mailman's hat squatted on a buckled mattress crammed between the walls of the shed. Around him, stacked cardboard boxes, overflowing ragged clothes, and newspaper threatened to topple.

"The Pan's *gone*," the man said.

"He's dead?"

"Dead? Sheeit! That old bastard ain't never gonna die. Too mean, too crazy. Still getting it up. Health inspectors tried running him out for keeping ducks, roosters, whatnot downstairs. Then somebody come up here and massacre all his pigeons he been raising twenty years. He's *gone*, that's all."

They looked at the coops again, this time noticing clots of feathers, brownish stains, flecks of skin spattered on the wood and panes. Steve put the bottle back in the bag.

"Do you live in *there?*" Dove asked.

"Come on in, my man. Have a look around." The man grinned, showing bad teeth, gesturing like a doorman.

"We gotta go," Steve said. "Sorry to bother you."

"Hey, what about your grandma? You really want duck's blood?"

"She makes soup with it."

"Maybe I can get you some."

"You know where Pan Gowumpe moved to?"

"Maybe I do." He took his mailman's hat off and rubbed his hand over woolly gray hair. His scalp showed through like varnished wood. "Cost you a buck."

"Okay," Steve agreed, "But you get us there first."

The small man turned back and groped in the shed for a leather mail sack. He slung it over his shoulder and clamped a padlock on the shed door. "We go this way," he said, raising a trapdoor from the roof.

They followed him down the alleys, waiting while he stopped to examine garbage cans, stuffing empty pop bottles in his mail pouch.

"Were you a mailman?" Dove asked.

"I *am* the Mailman. That's what folks around here call me. Nobody messes with the U.S. Mail."

He stopped at a dumpster behind a supermarket. Flies swarmed from crates as he picked through spoiled peaches, stuffing wilted lettuce and carrots into his sack. "You gotta live off the city same way country people live off the land. Like the rat does. You ever eat garbage?"

"Only when he makes me," Dove said, pointing to Steve.

"You make your little brother eat garbage?"

"It's just a threat," Steve said.

"Wait'll you guys are old. Won't be no threat. Don't matter if you're white or red or black—you'll eat what you can get. Garbage, dog food, even drink duck's blood." He started to laugh. "How sick your grandma anyway?"

"She thinks she's dying."

"And this duck soup gonna cure that? Man, I gotta get me some."

"Gimme dat *zupa, zupa, zupa,*" Dove started singing.

"That's good," the Mailman said, and started singing along with him.

They sang until they reached the end of the alley. Cars whished by. Across the street, Douglass Park stretched for blocks. It had been in the news the summer before when a riot followed a fight between a white softball team and a black one.

"You sure this is the way to Gowumpe's?" Steve asked.

"Shortcut," the Mailman said.

A group of black guys, playing softball behind a rickety backstop, ignored them as they entered the park. The Mailman led them into the trees, down a path that twisted through a dense jungle of bushes. When they could see the lagoon sparkling through a gap in the bushes he motioned them down. Together they crawled to the edge of the lagoon and crouched where it got soggy, behind a screen of reeds and cattails. Out toward the middle, beyond the lily pads, a family of white ducks glided.

"*Zupa*," the Mailman whispered, grinning.

"Christsake," Steve said, under his breath, "you're crazy. You said you were taking us to Pan Gowumpe's."

"Not exactly. I said I could get you duck's blood. Look, I know the Pan. He treats them birds like family. He ain't gonna give you shit, nohow. Whole time I knowed him he ain't give me nothin' but an egg now and then—him healthy and me starvin'." He fished into his mail pouch and came up with a handful of dried bread crusts. "People throw these out for the birds—there's folks throw away their entire lives. You gotta start learning to see what's around you for the taking."

He snapped off a corner of bread and skimmed it out so that when it touched, a circle spread on the water as if a fish had been feeding.

"They're turning," Dove said.

"Course they are. Ducks know what a free meal is. Now, don't make no noise."

He continued flipping bread out. They crouched, watching the ducks racing one another to gobble it down. Each throw brought them a little closer to shore.

The Mailman carefully emptied the sack out between his legs and handed it to Steve, who was trying to see what had been in it.

"When I get the ducks outa the pond you get between them and the water and pounce this over one. You gotta be quick 'cause they already gun-shy from kids throwing rocks at 'em."

He was tossing bread near the shore now and began to creep backward, laying a trail of crusts. Two of the more aggressive ducks were already paddling at the mossy edge of the lagoon.

Steve held himself rigid among the reeds. Up that close their white feathers dazzled as if the sun were beating harder. He could see the scales on their vibrant orange webbing as they waddled, squishing, over mud. He was sweating, dizzy with the scorched smell of cattails, his eyes seeming to magnify the tiny pond world so that he could see the wake that water spiders left in the scum, translucent minnows darting through his reflection, turquoise bands on damsel flies. Something had gone wrong with the day. He felt disconnected, as he did sometimes walking to the dentist with Dove when he'd realize it would be so simple to turn around and not go. But he wouldn't turn and it would be like someone else still walking in his body. Then he thought of Busha—a vision of her struggling for breath in that shade-drawn room cluttered with photographs and holy pictures like frozen scenes from her life. Why did she want to go on living? But when he thought that his stomach knotted. He wanted her to live. The world would be too unnatural without her.

"Now, boy!" the Mailman whispered.

Steve sprang up and the ducks erupted in a flurry of feathers. The big drake he lunged for flapped past his shins, almost knocking him down. Two ducklings were trapped a moment between him and Dove and the Mailman, who were shooing with their arms, and when one of them tried squirting past him for the water he pounced with the sack.

The Mailman let out a whoop. "Told you I'd get us a duck, boy!"

They crouched, breathing hard, around the sack. The duck quacked worriedly inside. Steve's legs felt drained of strength.

"It's the littlest one," Dove said.

"We ain't gonna roast him," the Mailman said.

"What are we gonna do?"

"Carry a knife?"

"No," Steve said.

"Got the jar but no knife, eh?" The Mailman looked at him scornfully.

"We better let him go," Dove said. His voice quavered; his face was flushed. Steve could see he didn't like what was going on.

"What about your grandma's soup? Gonna let her die?"

Dove looked down, as if he were studying the weeds. The Mailman went over to the pile of junk he'd dumped out of his sack and picked up a Seven-Up bottle. He rapped it against a rock half submerged in the reeds. It didn't break. He smacked it again. It still didn't.

"We're not gonna kill it?" Dove whispered to Steve.

The Mailman was still rapping the bottle. Suddenly, it shattered, leaving him holding the jagged neck.

"Sheeit! A man could cut his finger off." He came over and handed it to Steve. "Hold this a second."

Steve set it down in the grass. The Mailman was slowly lifting up an end of the sack, squinting in. A stream of liquid green jetted out.

"Yah!" he yelped, flinching and falling backward into a sitting position. "I'm blinded!"

The duck had its tail end out, trying to wriggle free,

spurting a steady stream of green. Dove and Steve were trying to stuff the bird back under the sack.

"Man, what you doin' with that duck?" a voice drawled.

Four black teenagers stood on the path. They all had baseball gloves and the guy speaking was holding a bat.

"Who told you honkies you could come to our pond and steal a duck?" he asked. "This here's a black park. Ain't you got no respect? I'm asking you a question, honkie."

"I got respect," Steve said. It sounded phony as soon as he said it.

"You got sheeit, that's what you got." He walked over to the pile of bottles and rotten vegetables the Mailman had emptied, and scattered them about with the bat. "Been stealing our garbage, I see. You dudes are litterbugs too."

The other three guys laughed.

"Say now, son," the Mailman said. He was still dabbing his eyes with the tail of his shirt.

"Ain't *your* son, you crazy old nigger. What you doin' bringin' this white cheese here? I heard about you when I was little. They used to say you come at night for kids to stuff 'em in your mail sack. Goddamn, I oughta bust yo' head." He cocked the bat, then whirled on Steve. "Empty out your pockets, man."

Steve turned them inside out. One of the guys picked up the money and dropped it into his baseball mitt. The guy with the bat flicked two fingers into Steve's shirt pocket and lifted out his pack of Kools.

"You too young to smoke," he said. "Goddamn! Picking on defenseless animals. Man, I oughta kick your white asses from here to the Anticruelty Society. In fact, that's exactly what we gonna do unless you get your ass outa here *now*. And I mean run, motherfuckers!"

They ran, stumbling through the bushes when they lost the path, then out across the shaggy outfield grass.

"Hold up," the Mailman yelled, nearly collapsing when they reached the infield. He was panting hard and holding his heart. They waited for him to catch up, then helped him over to a park bench under the shade of a tree, across from a bus stop.

"One of them dollars was mine, goddamn!" He leaned his head back. One of his nostrils was leaking blood and there was green duckshit on his collar. "I'm a sick man. I needed that *zupa.* I need a cure."

"They didn't get the jar," Dove said. He handed it to Steve, the paper bag twisted and sweaty from his fist.

A bus pulled up and a few of the people stared.

"We gotta get out of here," Steve whispered. "It's getting late."

"Okay," the Mailman said, "I'll take you to Gowumpe's. It ain't that far."

They cut between the shells of condemned buildings, their broken windows clouded with plaster dust, and inside, the remains of rooms—overturned tables, flattened couches—amid the wreckage of fallen ceilings, as if the people who'd lived there had left in a hurry. Steve kept looking for something familiar to help them find their way back. He wasn't exactly lost, but disoriented about what streets to take. He didn't want Dove or the Mailman to know.

The Mailman led them to a backyard crowded with junked cars, weeds sprouting through hoodless engines.

"He lives up there," the Mailman said, pointing to the third floor of a building that almost touched the El tracks. All its windows were smashed out.

"Nobody lives in there," Steve said. "It's ready to fall down."

"Told you he's *gone*, boy. I watched him move in there. He tried to shake me, but I followed him. Look at that."

"What?"

"Pigeons."

Pigeons lined the tracks. Once he noticed them, Steve realized he'd been hearing them coo. They fluttered back and forth between the tracks and the windowsills on the third floor.

"See how they goes inside? Pigeons don't ordinarily go inside. Go on up."

"Ain't you coming with us?"

"We wouldn't get nothin' if I did. See, we had a little disagreement over whose pigeons they were at the other place, me living on the roof and all. The Pan think I called the health inspectors on him. Like I told you, he's *gone.* You go. I'm gonna be waiting right out here for you. Don't forget what you owe me neither."

"You saw they got my money."

"I'll settle for some of that *zupa.* I'll go home with you guys and when your grandma makes it you sneak some out for me."

"That wasn't our deal."

"Then I'll go back with you to get my dollar."

They shoved the unhinged door aside and Steve and Dove started up the stairs. As soon as they got beyond the sunlight from the doorway it was hard to see. The stairs were covered with rubble.

"Careful," Steve said, "there's no banister."

The Mailman was hissing something after them, but they couldn't quite hear him and didn't stop.

"I think he said he'd curse us if we tried to screw him," Dove whispered.

They reached the second floor just as the stairs began to rumble. The walls shook and plaster rained down. There was a roar. They could actually feel as well as hear the El go by.

"The tracks must almost be touching this wall," Steve said.

The train's echoes clattered behind as they walked down the second-floor hallway, past old rooms with sooty wallpapered walls. The doors had been removed. Light filtered in through broken-out windows facing west, sun nearly at eye level and blinding as if the suspended particles of dust were tiny mirrors. They entered one of the rooms and stared out the window, directly even with the El tracks. Pigeons were resettling in the wake of the train. They were pecking at something scattered among the ties.

"It's close enough to climb out and jump to the tracks. Hey, we can jump from here, then run down the tracks before the next train comes and make it to the next station, climb up on the platform and take the train home without paying." Steve boosted his leg over the windowsill as if he were climbing out.

"Don't do it," Dove pleaded.

"You must think I'm crazy."

"Listen," Dove said. "Hear that? It sounds like a snake charmer."

"It's a clarinet."

They followed the sound up to the third floor.

"It's wedding music," Dove whispered.

Steve had recognized it too. He didn't know the name of the song, but the words went "*Oh, how we danced on the night we were wed.*" The melody was Gypsylike and whenever it was played at weddings the old people danced with dreamy looks on their faces and sometimes wept if they were drunk. He knocked softly at the door it was coming from. The playing stopped. He knocked again, a little harder. No answer.

"Mr. Gowumpe, Antek from Joe's butcher shop said you could sell us some duck's blood for soup."

He knocked again. He explained, talking at the keyhole, about his grandmother. It was totally silent on the other side of the door except for the cooing of pigeons.

"Pretend you're walking away, down the stairs," Steve whispered to Dove. "Make a lot of noise."

"Sorry to bother you," he said loudly to the door. "Good-bye."

Dove stomped off. Steve flattened himself against the wall by the door. He could hear creaking movement on the other side, then the doorknob clicking quietly open. An enormous bushy head of white cowlicks peeked out, looking down the stairs.

"Mr. Gowumpe," Steve said.

The man jumped and slumped back against the doorjamb, sliding down, clutching the top button of the long underwear he wore. Dove came running back upstairs just as the man was crawling back inside. He rolled over heavily and lay on the floor beside his metal clarinet.

"You gave him a heart attack," Dove said.

The man lay there staring blankly at the ceiling. The floor was spread with newspapers splotched by bird droppings and weighed down with bricks. A torn bedspread hung over one window, tinting the late-afternoon light rose. The old man crossed his arms over his chest and closed his eyes.

"Mr. Gowumpe, Mr. Gowumpe," Steve said. "Are you all right? Should we go for a doctor?"

A huge white goose waddled out of another room and nuzzled the old man with his beak.

The man opened his eyes. Beneath his shaggy white eyebrows they were the blue of a gas flame. He grimaced, showing his teeth, and at that moment the goose said in a voice very much like a parrot's, "Doctor? Doctor? What does doctor know?"

The goose continued opening and closing its beak, but no more words came out.

The man had sat up. "He right," he said, nudging the goose. "Even if sick I don't need doctor. I look sick to you?"

"Why are you lying on the floor?" Dove asked.

"Nice floor. Besides, you give me little scare, I give you little scare."

Fowl were strutting across the room now—iridescent

roosters, speckled hens, white ducks. Pigeons landed on the sill and perched, cooing and swiveling metallic throats.

"Can you make the goose talk again?" Dove asked.

Gowumpe grimaced again, teeth looking powerful as a horse's, and the parrot voice came out of the goose. As soon as the goose heard it, it began to open and close its beak. "Why your *busha* sick? Just old?"

"It started when she fell down the stairs and broke her hip."

Gowumpe began to laugh. "*Czarnina* no fix that," he sputtered. "It's thick stuff, but you can't make cast from it. Can't make miracle either. When time to die, then time to die." With each burst of laughter the birds circled faster. "Maybe if you make soup out of Christ's blood. Ever see old ladies kissing relics? Blessing throats with candles, blessing eyes, ears. Hey, nobody blesses asshole. Why not? Has its troubles too." He'd changed back to the goose's voice. "How you find me?

"The Mailman showed us," Steve said.

"Mailman! Hey, he dirty, thiefing sumnabitch!"

"He's sick too," Dove said. "He needs some soup too."

"Ain't goddamn sick. He been cursed. Crazy old lady in the old building put evil eye on him for snooping in her garbage. She think the Mailman Russian spy!" He exploded into laughter and the roosters began to circle the room again. "He think blood soup gonna help him get it up again, understand? Push-push. Soup gonna make him push-push." He was flushing red under his white mane, stamping the floor in time to his laughter. Every time he said "push-push" he worked the middle finger of his left hand in and out of the fist of his right. They could feel the walls quaking the hilarity back, then the floor shaking, plaster sifting from the ceiling. A flight of pigeons beat in through the window. Dove clapped his hands over his ears as the El roared by as loud as if the tracks had split the room. The air swam with plaster dust and feathers.

"Seventy-five! Seventy-five! That's how old Gowumpe!" He was cawing in the voice of the goose. "And still push-push!"

The train was racketing away. "How old you?" he asked, pointing at Dove.

"Nine."

"Nine, no push-push. Though possible! I'm still in Old Country when nine. Didn't know a damn ting. Nobody knows at nine. What you know?"

"Nothing," Dove said.

"See, what I tell you? How old you, *dupa*?" he asked Steve.

"Thirteen."

"Understand *dupa*?"

"It means 'behind,' " Steve said, " 'butt,' something like 'asshole.' "

"That's right. See, thirteen years and you know 'asshole.' Seventy-five years and what I know?"

"What?"

"More *dupa*."

He stomped across the room, gesturing for them to follow, chickens squawking out from under his feet. "Hey, pick up your feet over newspaper," he yelled at Steve and Dove.

"Glass doorknob." He pointed. "*Dupa* throne always behind the door with the glass doorknob." He flung the door open and grabbed Dove by the collar. "Look down, don't fall."

On the other side the floorboards jutted out a foot, then dropped three stories into darkness. Plumbing dangled from bare lathing. Gowumpe grinned, all the while grunting, lip-farting, pantomiming tremendous explosions.

"One day health inspector will be poking nose down there and killed by Gowumpe shit bomb!"

"You mean you really *go* hanging over the edge?" Dove asked, astonished.

"Show you something else." Gowumpe got down on his hands and knees, opening and closing his mouth repeatedly without making a sound. The goose waddled over immediately, its beak opening and closing in the same way, and with a short beat of its wings hopped to his back. Gowumpe crawled across the room to his silver clarinet, then slowly rose, the goose taking short steps up his spine, until he was standing straight with the goose perched on his head. He theatrically tilted his clarinet toward the ceiling and blew, and at the same time the goose extended its neck, honking in perfect pitch, spreading its wide, white wings.

Together, holding the note, wild white hair, white throat, white wings, they seemed to fill the room.

Dove and Steve applauded.

"Ten years together," Gowumpe said, raising his eyebrows toward the goose. "Goose older than you."

He stooped and the goose hopped back to the newspapers.

"What you got in the bag, little boy?" the goose asked.

Dove took the Miracle Whip jar out of the bag and showed it to the goose.

"Oh, yes, you're the little boy who wants some blood. Most little boys just want feathers."

"Boys, I tell you something," Gowumpe broke in. "I used to work in the Yards. You know? Armour, Wilson, Swift, all of them. Twenty years ago it was big ting. On Thursdays you could smell all over the city. People say, 'They're making soap. Making glue.' All these DPs working there—it's all right to say it, I'm DP too—Polacks, Lugans, Bohunks. People who knew how to be hungry. Surrounded by all that meat! Sometimes DP on the line would drink some blood. Fresh, right on the job. I see it. Think it would make them strong, cure hangover, good for push-push. Take jars home for women to keep them young. A lot of bullshit."

"She thinks it will help her," Steve said.

"No. You don't know yet. There are two kinds of people. Living people and dying people. Living people, they don't hardly know about dying people. They think there are just people. But dying people know there are two kinds. They know no other difference is important—man and woman, black and white, old and young—doesn't matter. Some feel angry, some ashamed, some try to pretend they living." He looked at both of them. "Ahccckk." He shook his head in disgust. "Hey," he said to Dove, "show you something more."

He led them into the next room, where the goose had come from. The floor was scattered with hard corn. Two old, four-legged, disconnected bathtubs stood in two corners, half full of water and bobbing ducklings. Ducks waddled across wet newspaper quacking. A huge, homemade birdcage, fashioned from chicken wire and screening and full of branches, was set against the wall. Canaries, parakeets, and finches flitted inside.

"People give me birds when they can't keep self," Gowumpe said. "Gotta find another place before it gets cold. Look here."

He carefully opened a door to a small bedroom. Boards had been hammered across its single window like horizontal bars so that the light streaked in leaving most of the room dim. The closet in the corner was doorless. Perched on a bare coatrack, a large, startlingly blue bird blinked. A scarlet crescent of feathers opened like a slash beneath its throat. Two tail streamers arced almost to the floor, their amethyst tips sweeping above the dropping-spattered pie plates of water and cut-up fruits buzzing with flies. It partially stretched its wings, revealing bald, raw skin among the brilliant plumage.

"Been pulling out his own feathers," Gowumpe whispered.

Suddenly the bird screamed so violently that Steve and Dove pulled the door shut.

"You gonna miss it," Gowumpe said, opening it and pushing them in to look.

Inside, the bird had ruffled itself to double its original size, blue plumes sheening bronze and green, radiating colors as it hung upside down, swinging wildly from the coatrack, its streamer tails whipping the air like antennae from some other world.

Gowumpe pushed them out and shut the door.

"What is it?"

"Don't know. Old lady, dentist's widow, give me."

They turned back to the main room with its newspaper and corn on the floor, but it looked different to Steve now. He couldn't shake off the image of the bird; its colors were superimposed on the gutted walls. Dove was dabbling his hand in the tub with the ducklings.

"You still want?" Gowumpe asked, pointing to the jar as if Steve might have changed his mind.

"Yes," Steve said.

"How much money you got?"

"We got jumped in the park on the way here. But whatever it is I'll get it and come back."

"Robbed. I live here forty years—DPs, Mexicans, coloreds—and don't get robbed."

"What about your pigeons?"

"That was crazy person who did that." He took a shoebox off the windowsill. Silverware jangled. He lifted out a butcher knife.

"You come here again or tell someone where Gowumpe living and *shlshsh*," he said to Steve, running the knife past his own throat.

"We won't tell," Steve swore.

"You're not going to kill one," Dove said.

"No, they got little faucets."

They waited. Another El screamed past, filling the room with pigeons. Dove held his ears and turned his face to the wall till it passed. Finally, Gowumpe came out holding the bag in the palm of a big hand.

"Hold by bottom, too heavy. Feel how warm."

Dove wouldn't touch it. Gowumpe handed it to Steve.

"Thank you."

"Sure, *dziękuję*, like you care about old people. If Busha can't drink it get doctor to pump it in—stick tubes in her nose, tubes in arms, make her prisoner in old people's home. Nice guy. Okay, get outa here. I gotta take nap. Stay up half the night keeping rats away from birds."

"Good-bye," they said.

"Good-bye, Dupa Yash and Nothing Head," the goose cackled as the door closed.

They peered out across a narrow cinder alley into the dark underpinnings of the El tracks. Instead of going back down the way they'd come, they'd used the exit at the other end of the hall.

"The Mailman must still be waiting at the other door," Steve whispered. "As soon as a train goes over we'll run across under the tracks. As long as we follow them it'll get us home."

"We promised him some," Dove said.

"He can get his own. Jesus Christ! You want him following us?"

"What if he sees us?"

"Just keep running."

"If he catches me are you gonna stop?"

"He's not gonna catch you, asshole, if you keep running. He's too old. Get ready."

They could hear the train, still blocks away, rumbling toward them, then it was streaming overhead and they clambered over a downed cyclone fence and sprinted across the alley.

It was like entering a forest of girders. Light came in slats through the tracks above, throwing the bleached shadow of tracks before them. The girders crisscrossed at intervals, forcing them to flip the V center of beams. Steve cradled the jar against him like a football. His shirt was sweaty and stuck to the paper bag. They kept looking back. If the Mailman was following them along the girders they couldn't see him. But the shadows moved. They kept jogging.

Rush-hour trains hurtled in both directions, coming at shorter intervals, soot and sparks showering down. The air smelled scorched with the friction of screeching steel and the hiss of pneumatic brakes.

"Here it comes." Dove kept yelling as each train pursued them; yelling as if they were actually running on the tracks instead of the shadows of tracks, and were being overtaken and crushed in the deafening roar when the slats of light above were blotted out to mere laser flashes between cars. Steve glanced back. Dove was running with his hands over his ears, his mouth gaping. Steve couldn't hear if his brother was screaming.

The tracks followed the alley, running above its blackened walls, broken backyard fences, and wash hanging from dirty lines. The cross streets were crowded with people coming home from work, coming alive for night—neon blinking on in stores, music blasting from bars. So long as Steve and Dove stayed under the tracks it was as if they were invisible.

By the time they hit Twenty-second, Steve knew they were safe. He was a block ahead of Dove, so he sat on a girder to wait for him to catch up. He knew he should have felt more winded, but he didn't. He felt he could continue running for miles. He was thinking of coming home with the blood, of making the soup, of the house filling with his aunts and uncles, everyone drinking and joking, the washtub brimming with ice and cans of beer and pop floating in the freezing water.

"I can't run anymore," Dove said, slumping down on the girder. "Which side is the appendix on?"

"The other one."

Another train went over. Dove clapped his hands over his ears and closed his eyes.

"Recognize where we are?" Steve asked. "There's the dentist's office." It was a four-story tan-brick building. In the dusky light the bricks looked pink. "Wanta stop by for a filling or two? Come on, we can take the Alley Heartaches from here."

They walked down Twenty-second, past the dentist's, and cut down a gangway into the alley. The sky was lilac over the backyard trees.

"I banged my ankle on a girder," Dove said, stopping to pull down his sock.

"You'll live. Stop faking."

"I'm not," Dove mumbled, limping.

"We got it!" Steve yelled at him. He started strutting and singing:

"Gimme dat *zupa zupa zupa.*
Kick in the *dupa dupa dupa.*"

He was hopping along behind Dove, kicking him in the pants in time to the words. Dove trudged, head down, ignoring him. He wasn't sharing any of the elation Steve was feeling.

"Sing!" Steve said.

"Quit it!"

"A real sorehead. What's your problem?"

"We promised the Mailman. He was sick too. And what if he finds out where we live?"

"The Mailman!" Steve suddenly whirled around. "Holy shit! I just saw him duck behind us. Run!"

He took off full speed down the alley. Dove tried to keep up but quickly fell behind. Steve kept going. He wanted to run till he was out of breath, to burn up whatever was making his blood jump like electricity. Running always made him feel there were possibilities.

He wasn't anxious to go home, for the day to end, though he wished the explanations were over. The closer they got, the less real the celebration he'd imagined with his aunts and uncles became. There was a dread beneath his excitement he didn't want to face—a rising feeling of smallness and helplessness at the heart of his elation. He could visualize the Miracle Whip jar sitting for weeks in the refrigerator, the blood coagulating in the cold. By the time he reached the empty lot behind Baynor's Drugs he was breathing hard. He sat down in the high weeds behind the billboard that screened the lot from the street. He took the bottle out of the bag. It was plum-colored, not brownish, the way he remembered it. He wondered if the twilight was doing that. He unscrewed the cap slowly, took a deep breath of weed-scented air, then carefully sniffed the jar, ready to fight down nausea. It smelled like vinegar. There was a sweet, earthy smell beneath the sourness that was familiar. He took a drop on the end of his finger. It was too watery. Beets.

He tasted it.

Gowumpe had given him beet juice.

He sank back in the weeds and lay looking up at the wafer of moon solidifying over the garage roofs. He closed his eyes, trying to think of what he'd say when he got home, trying to think of Busha. But his mind kept drifting back to the strange bird burning with its own colors, living in a closet. He could hear Dove panting up the alley. He dipped his finger into the jar and drew a streak across his forehead, then screwed the cap on and put the jar into the torn bag. He lay back in the weeds, groaning, eyes half shut.

"The Butchie got me . . . the Butchie got me."

Dove was crying, holding his side.

"Go to hell! You bastard!"

"I'm hurt bad," Steve said, raising his head out of the weeds.

"Hey! You're bleeding! What should I do?"

"Get a priest. I'm dying."

"I'll get Baynor."

Steve jumped up, laughing.

Dove stood watching him wipe his head with leaves.

"You didn't fool me. There's no Butchie. The Mailman wasn't following us either."

"Quit faking. Admit it. You were crying. You thought they got me."

"You're the one always faking," Dove said.

Steve took the jar out of the bag. "Dare me to drop it?"

"Go ahead. It's Busha's."

"Think I won't?"

"Yeah."

"*You* save Busha."

He flipped the jar up over the garage roofs. It turned end over end against the fading sky and seemed to hang like a kicked football, then plunged down. Dove lunged forward to catch it, only to flinch as it touched his hands, jerking his elbows back into his stomach desperately as the jar hit the pavement with the muffled explosion of glass, splattering the cuffs of their jeans, the white laces of their gym shoes.

Neighborhood Drunk

Sterndorf always looked like he needed a shave. He'd be sprawled out, sunning himself and drinking from a bottle in a brown paper bag, in the Victory garden on the corner of Twenty-third. It wasn't really a garden, just a little patch of grass and dandelions on a concrete slope. The concrete had been painted red, white, and blue, but most of the red and blue had flaked away. There was a rusting flagpole set in a white star in the center and a plaque inscribed with the names of all the men in the neighborhood who'd been killed in the war.

I used to play on it when my grandpa would take me for walks. I remember holding on to the flagpole with one hand and spinning around the points of the star till I was dizzy. Grandpa would usually stop there and sit down. Something about Sterndorf made him seem like an old man to me even then, though his shaggy hair was still blond. It seemed natural for him and Grandpa to talk and joke, passing the bottle back and forth.

Once, the Good Humor man came peddling by and Sterndorf bought me a banana popsicle, so cold the paper stuck when he broke it in half against the edge of the plaque with his shaky hands.

Danny's grandfather, his *dzia dzia*, came shuffling up.

"Here comes the draft dodger," Grandpa said. Danny's *dzia dzia* always told the same story in broken English about how he came to America because he didn't want to be in the czar's army.

"Gimme bite," he said, addressing my popsicle, not me.

We all started laughing. He didn't have any teeth.

We'd never stay too long. The family would get down on Grandpa for drinking on the street.

"People notice, people talk," my mother would tell him.

Every time we went out for walks past the Victory garden I'd watch for people noticing and talking about us. But since it was the middle of the morning with everyone at work there were only the old ladies, dressed in long black coats and babushkas, even in summer, coming back from church.

⁂

It was the year after my grandpa died. I was standing in the backyard crying because my mother had made me wear short pants.

Sterndorf snuck up on me, peering in over the wire fence. He'd been walking down the alley. He always walked through alleys. He wanted to know what I was doing.

"I'm a hunter," I told him, shooting with a stick, pretending I'd been playing.

"You be the native and I'll be the lion," he said. He dumped out a boxful of garbage and tossed it in the yard. Then he climbed up on the garbage cans and jumped over the fence. "Here's your shield." He handed me the empty box, flies flying out of it.

I brandished my stick like a spear and crouched behind my shield. Sterndorf got down on all fours and began to growl, ferociously shaking his manelike head.

His roaring attracted my mother. She came running out, potato masher in hand, just as he was butting his head against the box, hopping up and down and pawing at me. I was jabbing back with the stick.

"What in the hell!" she said.

But when Sterndorf scrambled up and ran for the fence she started to scream.

He tried to flip it one-handed but his cuff caught as he went over and toppled him into the alley.

"Ma!" I said.

She whirled around and clunked the potato masher off the top of my head.

Sterndorf, ripped trousers flapping, took off down the alley.

"I called the police," the lady next door yelled from her second-story window.

"That's just great," my mother said under her breath, glaring at me.

Later, a squad car pulled up in front of our house, blue light blinking and police calls crackling. My mother went out to talk to the cops. Sterndorf was handcuffed in the backseat. The car was surrounded by people staring in like they'd never seen him before.

I tried to avoid Sterndorf. He looked more and more like Struwwelpeter, a monster from a German fairy tale, with black, overgrown fingernails and wildly sprouting hair. But I felt guilty passing him without nodding hello. He probably didn't know what was going on around him anyway.

One lunch hour he staggered through the schoolyard, a brown strand of drool swinging from his stubbly chin as he tried to shake it off. He stood throwing up on the volleyball court with the kids running and screaming around him. The nuns herded us inside. "There, but for the grace of God, go I," they told us.

Sometimes he'd do something crazy like wrapping himself up in the funnies section of the Sunday paper and going to sleep in the middle of California Avenue during rush hour. The cops would come and haul him away. Another time the hook and ladder had to come and get him down from the high-voltage wires at the top of an electric pole where he'd spent the day drinking, swearing, and spitting down on whoever stopped below.

They never locked him up for long. In a week he'd usually reappear, looking cleaned up, talking with the neighborhood men in the evenings as they drank their beer and watered their small lawns.

The only job he had was mopping up in various neighborhood taverns. He didn't need much. The Army sent him a check and he lived with his mother in a small house she owned on Luther Street. Like most of the other old people, his mother came from the Old Country. She was hard to tell apart from the other women, all wearing the same dark clothes as if they were constantly going to funerals, kneeling together in the front pews facing the golden tiers of vigil candles burning under the icon of Our Lady of Częstochowa, murmuring the Rosary in mournful, nasal chorus long after mass was over.

⌘

It was the summer Sterndorf started playing softball with us. No one knew why, but he'd show up and ask to get into the game. He'd stand at home plate, cigarette dangling from his lip, waving the bat around, scraggly hair flashing from his armpits, pimpled shoulders sunburned pink, but the rest of him still alkie white.

He ran the bases like a maniac, sliding whether he had to or not, bouncing up dusty, yelling, "You guys catch that slide?" He played outfield the same way, racing in under flies, tripping over his droopy trousers, shouting, "I got it, I got it," arms flailing everyone away. By July he'd started catching the ball.

We were all hanging around outside Kozak's sipping Cokes and pitching pennies after a game, watching George's big brother, Pancho, driving his motorcycle around the block. It was a huge black Harley, gleaming with chrome and reflectors, its saddlebags almost touching the street. It sounded like an airplane taking off, leaving a wake of dust and papers every time he wheeled the corner. George said Pancho had just been drafted for Korea and was trying to sell the bike.

"He wants to learn to fly a copter while he's in," George bragged. "Says he's glad his number came up before he killed himself around here."

We all laughed. Pancho had a reputation for not backing down.

"Don't look too *glad* to me," Sterndorf said. He'd been sitting there drinking a Kayo. He hadn't been getting drunk lately.

"When it's your turn to fight, you gotta fight," Tarbull said.

"Let me at 'em," Sterndorf said, jumping up, fists cocked, struggling as if some invisible force were holding him back. "Who we fightin'?"

"Ever hear of the Commies?" Tarbull asked him. He had a bubble-gum-card collection of Korean War battles.

Sterndorf cupped his armpit with his hand and pumped his arm up and down so it sounded like his armpit was farting.

"You ever hear what they do to our guys when they take them prisoner?" Tarbull said. "Use them for bayonet practice. Pull out their intestines and tie them around their legs, then make them run races. Not just soldiers either, nuns and priests too."

"They taught me the same crap when I was in school too. You know the Commies were our allies when I was in?"

"Hey, you ought to join up again," Dan said.

"Naw, he's gonna come back to school with us."

"He's gonna be out there running the bases in the snow."

We were all laughing and Sterndorf was laughing too.

"I used to bury the dead guys when I was in. Anybody ever tell you how they mark them at the front? They wedge the dog tags between their upper and lower teeth and then kick the jaws shut."

"Bullshit!" George said.

"Hell, yeah! One guy was sleepin' off a drunk and they thought he was dead. *Kapow!*" Sterndorf lay down on the sidewalk snoring. He took a bottle cap and stuck it between his teeth, then jumped up, trying to pry his jaws apart, marching around in a circle, saluting with one hand and pointing to his mouth with the other.

Dan put his thumb in his bottle of pop, shook it up, and squirted him.

"Got me," Sterndorf said through gritted teeth.

It was like a signal—suddenly we were all squirting him

from every direction, making noises like machine guns.

Sterndorf was groaning, spinning around, and grabbing places all over his body as if the bullets were going in, staggering into the street like a dying gunfighter at the end of a movie just as Pancho came tearing around the corner. Sterndorf made a dive back for the sidewalk. The motorcycle caught his leg and snapped his body around—as if he were still clowning—but when he came down his head hit the curb. He didn't even have his arms out in front. It sent a vibration through the sidewalk, through the soles of my gym shoes and into my teeth. He just lay there.

Pancho kept on going.

"Jesus!" Tarbull said. He and I went running in the store to get Mr. Kozak.

They called an ambulance, but it took a while for it to come. Meanwhile Mr. Kozak and his brother ran out and turned him over. Sterndorf screamed. His ankle was broken but no one realized it at the time because of his head. His eyebrow had disappeared and the bone behind it gleamed white. I turned away. They were holding him down and he was moaning and trying to get up.

A crowd gathered. Someone had gone for Sterndorf's mother. Everyone fell back to let her through. She was small and wrinkled. She knelt beside him, legs as thin as rods sticking out from the hem of her dress, her lips moving as if she were praying, but she hadn't had time to put in her teeth, so it looked like chewing. She had a little handkerchief out and was trying to wipe some of the blood where it pooled in his eye. When it got soaked she wrung it out.

By the time the ambulance came Sterndorf was half sitting up with a bloody towel pressed against his head. They got him on the stretcher, his mother pleading with the attendants, "You take to VA? You take to VA?"

She'd touched her face with her hands and looked as if

she'd been in the accident too. They hauled both of them into the ambulance, slammed the doors on her terrified face, and shrieked away.

We went over to the curb to watch Mr. Kozak take a bucket of water and slosh the blood toward the sewer.

⁂

Sterndorf disappeared after the accident. He no longer talked with the men hosing their grass at dusk or drank with the weekend crowd. The softball teams from Bud's Lounge and 24 Lanes had disbanded and most of his old buddies were gone.

He mopped up at Eddie's Edelweiss Tap after it closed at four A.M. Sometimes he'd still be out around nine in the morning, his arms always looking freshly scalded up to the elbows.

He was still usually drunk, but he'd stopped clowning. The sirens of squad cars, fire trucks, and ambulances no longer signaled his existence.

Once, he reminded the neighborhood how crazy he used to be by walking the streets singing "It Ain't Gonna Rain No More" at the top of his raspy voice at three in the morning the day after his mother's funeral, till somebody yelled shut up.

He lived alone in her house after she died. Everyone expected him to burn himself up in it. He'd stay shut up weeks at a time. Little kids would go over and peek in to see if he was dead yet. One day he painted all the windows with orange house paint so nobody could see in. Then, on a sweltering summer night, he tried to open them and couldn't because they were painted stuck. So he bashed his kitchen windows out, throwing house bricks through from the outside. Later he nailed a bedspread over them.

After that he never used the front door. He'd come down the alley and climb in through the broken back windows. People said sometimes he'd play the radio loud and dance by himself in the alley and supposedly he cried once from two A.M. to six in the morning. Whatever he did, he did at night, which is why the little kids nicknamed him the Count and made up stories about him coming to their windows to suck their blood.

Maybe they were one reason he'd stay in during the day. They'd follow him whenever he'd limp out, shouting, "The Count!" He didn't look anything like Dracula—bent over as if he had a constant stomachache, clothes ragged, skin jaundiced. They threw stones and garbage, tormented him as we never had. Perhaps he was so ugly they really were afraid.

The summer we were fifteen, Dan discovered an old suitcase of his father's full of liqueur miniatures. The suitcase had been sitting on the back porch for years and it was like coming on a hidden treasure chest. They looked like jewels, exquisite shapes of glass glowing ruby, amber, crème-de-menthe emerald.

We'd sneak back there on June evenings with the light out in the kitchen and Dan's parents in the front of the apartment watching TV. I had a penlight and we'd study their labels before sampling. It brought the world into our lives as no geography book ever could. From necks narrower than a straw drops of exotic places burned on our tongues: Cognac, Chartreuse, Curaçao.

My family took a Labor Day trip to Wisconsin that summer and let me stay over at Dan's. Dan, George, and I were sitting around my empty apartment playing cards and smoking cigars when we got the idea of buying our own bottle. We were too young-looking, but we'd heard about getting winos to do it, so we pooled our money and went looking for Sterndorf.

"Suppose he tells our folks," George said.

We stopped. That July we'd cut George in on the miniatures and he'd responded by inviting us to sample stuff from their basement bar on his father's bowling nights. After we poured our drinks he'd fill the bottles back up to their original levels with water. When his father finally caught on he threatened to tear George's arms off if he caught him drinking again before he was eighteen. Nobody doubted he meant it either; his father had become kind of violent ever since Pancho had been killed.

"Why should he tell on us?"

"Yeah, stop worrying," Dan said.

I was feeling tense now, and half hoped we wouldn't find Sterndorf. We matched pennies to see who'd ask him. Dan lost and I felt better.

Sterndorf was sitting on the pipe fence in front of Eddie's Edelweiss, watching the traffic. It was dark already and the neon sign with its burned-out letter E flickered between red and pink, attracting hordes of crackling little brown moths. We checked out the situation, then walked over to him. The flickering red light exaggerated the scar that started where an eyebrow should have been and dented up into his forehead. His eyes stared back, unaligned, flaky around the rims and runny.

"How would you like to make yourself some money?" Dan asked in his most condescending tone.

"What ya want me to buy ya?" Sterndorf said.

We looked at one another, relieved.

"How much will it cost us?"

"How much ya got?"

"Four and a quarter."

"Cost ya a quarter."

Dan looked at us for approval. "Okay."

"Well, what yas want?"

"A fifth of brandy," Dan said, pronouncing "brandy" very distinctly.

"All you got enough for's rotgut." He rasped a couple of times. It looked like he was laughing. "You boys gonna have a little party?" The longer we stood there, the more I could smell him—the sourness of alcohol and beneath it a mustiness like something spoiled.

"A friendly little gathering," Dan was saying.

"Walk in the alley after me," Sterndorf said. We watched him drag himself away, stooped and shuffling his feet as if they were wrapped in bandages. He disappeared into the alley and we followed him.

"Look," he said, "I'm gonna do you guys a favor. Loan yas enough to buy a fifth." He fished in his trousers and came out with a couple of bills that looked like they'd been used for Kleenex. "They could put me away for this, you know that?"

"Sure," Dan said. His voice broke.

"A fifth ain't nothin' with three guys," Sterndorf said.

"We know."

"Well, what yas want? Want Beam?"

"Sure, Beam's fine."

"Well, gimme the money."

"Oh, yeah." Dan hurriedly dug it out. He dropped a quarter and we listened to it roll around somewhere in the shadow of a garage. We got down to find it.

"For crissakes forget it," Sterndorf said. "Wait here."

We waited, not saying much. Dan lit a cigarette.

"You want the cops to see us here?" George said.

Dan looked at him, then crushed it out.

"Why's he loaning us money?" George said. He was whispering.

"He just doesn't know what he's doing," I said.

"Maybe he ain't comin' back."

"He tries that and we'll roll him," Dan said.

We saw him approaching with the streetlight behind him. He handed the bag to Dan.

"Thanks," we said.

"Don't forget to pay me back."

"Sure thing." We took off down the alley. Dan handed me the bottle and I stuffed it under my shirt. We started running.

❖

We were playing for drinks. Whoever had the best hand drank the shot in the middle of the table. When I'd win I'd brace myself before I could swallow it. I could feel it roll all the way down my throat, past my heart and leave it beating, then settle in my stomach. I was sweating and opened up my shirt. We were all talking loud, swearing, laughing like crazy. The whiskey kept going down in the bottle. I never thought we'd kill it, but we were doing it. Dan took the deck of cards and threw them in the air. *Fifty-two-card pickup*! They floated slowly to the carpet. I could see their faces as they fell. George knocked the bottle of ginger ale on the rug and it lay there in a fizzing puddle. We almost got hysterical laughing over it. Then it occurred to me that it was my house we were wrecking.

"Let's get some air," I said. When I stood my shoulders swung wonderfully loose, like they were on hinges.

We were weaving down the streets. They looked like different streets. The moon was too bright to look at.

"What time is it?" George asked.

"It's not late," I said.

"My old man's gonna tear my arms off." He chuckled.

We walked underneath the viaduct on Rockwell. Dan was kicking cracked slabs of cement off the walls and smashing them into the yellow light bulbs that glowed along the ceiling.

"My old man's gonna kill me."

"He'll tear your balls off," Dan said.

"I'm too drunk to go home," George said.

"We're bombed!" Dan yelled, his voice amplified by the echoing viaduct. He smashed another bulb, glass raining down on us. "Screw everything!" he shouted.

Dan couldn't seem to pop the last bulb. It glared back, unbreakable. He reached into a girder and pulled out an empty wine bottle.

"Watch this!" He hurled it like a hand grenade into the light bulb.

"I'm hit, I'm hit," George yelled. His hands covered his face. A car rumbled through, its headlights shining down the scrawled walls. We froze, but it kept going.

"I thought it was the cops," Dan said.

We stepped out into the moonlight.

"Is it bleeding?" George asked. He took his hands away.

"There's nothing there."

"God! What a wimp," Dan said.

We were walking down the boulevard. Cars whished by, headlights and taillights streaked together. George fell into a hedge and couldn't get up. Dan got involved in stamping out someone's flower garden.

I wondered if I could jump the hedges and realized I was running at them. They knocked my legs out from under me and softly dumped me on my head. The grass felt wet and cool. I just wanted to lie there—me at the little end of the telescope, the moon at the other. I could feel the planet spinning, the centrifugal force pushing me down into the velvet earth.

"Are you okay?" Dan was shouting.

"Great."

"You did a triple somersault."

We turned down Twenty-fourth. The lights were out in all the houses. I'd never realized what a wonderful time this was to be up. The streets were ours. We turned into an alley and stood facing a fence.

"You're getting it on my shoes," Dan yelled at George.

"I gotta get home."

"Well, go on, then, for crissake!"

"My old man'll be waitin' up for me." George turned away.

"Hey," Dan said, "he's cryin'!"

"No, he's not. Right, George?"

Dan turned around and pissed on my shoe.

"You did that purposely, asshole." I zipped my pants up, then took the lid off a garbage can and flung it at his head. He ducked and it crashed against the fence. He swung and caught me in the nose. I missed with a huge uppercut. We were reeling and punching and ducking.

"Wait," Dan said. "Time out." He leaned against the phone pole. His tongue stuck out. "Ahhhgc," he gagged.

"You got a bloody nose," George said.

"Big deal."

We were standing there watching Dan puke. Sterndorf came limping past him out of the shadows of the narrow alley. He was laughing his phlegm-rattled laugh.

"You got a bloody nose," he said.

"No shit?"

"You guys havin' a ball? We're all together on a drunk," he said.

"Who's drunk?"

Sterndorf squinted at me, chuckling. He pointed at Dan. "You boys just ain't learned to hold your booze yet. Wait'll your stomachs get broke in."

He was laughing to himself as if he were trying to hold it in, the effort doubling him up, forcing snot out of his nose, making him laugh all the louder. His skin looked bluish under the streetlight. His head was thrown back and he was holding his crotch. I looked at George to see what he was making of it, but he was looking away, standing in a stupor. Sterndorf seemed out of control, laughing loud enough to wake up the entire neighborhood.

"Hey, Dan! Let's get going, man," I said.

Sterndorf lurched toward me and threw an arm around my neck, pushing his stubbly jaw against my ear as if he had some secret to share. But all he said was, "Who gives a shit? Who gives a shit?"

I stumbled backward, jerking away, and when he came at me again I twisted under his arm as if we were doing a dance and pushed him down. He sat down hard, spit something dark up on himself. Then got right up and came at me again and suddenly I was running and Sterndorf, who seemed like he could hardly walk, was chasing me. I could hear him breathing in fits and coughing right behind me and for a second was terrified he was going to catch me. I ran all out. Halfway down the alley I slowed down and turned around. He was far behind, still jogging along, and way down at the other end, silhouetted against the streetlight, I could see George and Dan. One of them was waving.

✣

We never paid him back. The next day, Dan and I sat around sipping tomato juice, pretending to each other that we had hangovers. Sometime that week we went out and looked for him, but he wasn't at Eddie's. Later, after school had started again, we heard from Dan's father that the fire-department ambulance had rushed him to the VA hospital, that he'd been hemorrhaging "black blood" from his stomach, and that he was done for.

"That's what he threw up that night," I told Dan.

We couldn't figure out how he could have laughed so hard or run like that when he was dying.

"That's why he borrowed us the money,' Dan said.

"He might not have even known he was that sick, I argued. "He never knew half of what was going on."

But Dan was sure Sterndorf knew he was dying, because if he thought he was going to go on living for a while he would have needed every cent for his own booze.

Visions of Budhardin

The elephant was there, waiting in the overgrown lot where once long ago there had been a Victory garden, and after that a billboard, but now nothing but the rusting hulks of abandoned cars. The children grew silent as they gathered to inspect it: the crude overlapping parts, the bulky sides and lopsided rump, the thick squat legs that looked like five-gallon ice-cream drums, huge cardboard ears, everything painted a different shade of gray, and the trunk the accordion-ribbed hose from a vacuum cleaner. They stared back at Budhardin's eyes looking at them through the black sockets above the trunk. The holes were set too close together for a real elephant and made it look cross-eyed and slightly evil.

They couldn't see inside where Budhardin sat on a stool looking out at the world, his feet on pedals, hands manipulating levers, body connected to a network of lines and pulleys, a collar gripping his forehead for swinging the limp trunk, a clothesline tied around his waist running out the tail hole.

The children walked around, examining it from every angle.

"What in the fuck!" Billy Crystal said. He took his knife out and carved the date into the plaster rump and after it his initials, B.C.

Most of the kids chuckled even though they were familiar with the initials joke. A few threw stones, watching them bounce off, leaving dents in the paint job. Others had run across the lot to the alley, rumaged through the garbage cans, and began their bombardment of rotten tomatoes, banana peels, apple cores. Pedro "Chinga" Sanchez raced in balancing a glob of dogshit on a popsicle stick, arcing it as if it were a hand grenade. It splattered high off the humped back and was followed by a rain of beer cans and Petri wine bottles. Buddy Holly Shwartz sneaked up behind, grabbed the tail, and gave it a yank.

"Hey, it's just a goddamn clothesline!" he announced. They tried to light it up but nobody had any lighter fluid on him, so all they were able to do was get it smoking like a slow wick.

The elephant had closed its eyelids and stopped swinging its trunk from side to side. It stood perfectly still while they discussed pulling its trunk out by the roots or coming back with some gasoline to roast it.

"Ah, fuck it," Billy Crystal finally said, and they wandered off in little groups.

After they'd gone Mr. Ghazili, who owned the little combination grocery–candy store on the corner, shuffled over. As always, even in winter, he wore his house slippers, still speckled with pink paint from some job long ago. He stood looking up at the elephant, chewing his cigar. Little by little the elephant raised its lids.

"That's you in there, isn't it, Budhardin?" Ghazili said.

The elephant nodded its trunk.

"You might look a little different, but I'd recognize those eyes anywhere . . . same as used to stare up at me through the candy counter. Yeah, you liked them licorice whips. I remember the time you bought out my whole supply and went outside giving 'em away to all the kids telling 'em you were Jesus Christ. So they tied you to a phone pole and started beatin' you with them licorice whips. I had to run out there and untie you."

Two tears rolled down the elephant's face.

"Yeah, I remember . . . always alone . . . except for that friend—what was his name?—kid who got runned over . . . And now, a big tycoon! Yeah, I been readin' about you in the papers. Used to try and show people, but nobody around here's too interested in that kinda stuff, you know. Wouldn't of believed it was the same little fat kid anyway."

Budhardin didn't answer. He had failed to provide the elephant with a mouth.

"Your tail's smoking pretty bad back there," Mr. Ghazili said. He went around and rubbed the sparks out of the fibers. They stood looking at each other. Fistfuls of silver dollars, wristwatches, rings, suddenly issued from the trunk, spilling at Ghazili's feet.

"No, no," he said, "I don't want nothing. Just came by to say hello." He shuffled closer, his slippers crunching over the pile of coins, and patted the bump right above the elephant's trunk, then shuffled away.

Budhardin stood alone watching the day get older inside the sweltering body, wishing he could have told Ghazili the story. It was a story about two peasant boys on their own—their families dead, perhaps from plague. They find a huge plaster elephant standing in a field, left behind by a circus, and take to living in it. But the elephant is in poor repair and at night swarms of rats try to get in through the holes. During the day they wander about the deserted countryside scrounging for food. Once, they come upon a village, completely lifeless, with everything locked, and stare in through the bakery window at a fabulous display of cookies and frosted pastries.

He couldn't remember how it ended. It had been two years since the story had begun recurring in a series of haunting flashes and he still was unable to get beyond the two boys standing before the bakery window, their faces pressing against the glass. Sometimes people would say it sounded vaguely familiar, but, like him, they found it impossible to recall the ending.

He let his mind drift and found himself counting cars that passed. It was rush hour. He remembered how he and Eugene used to stand on the corner making endless surveys of cars. Long lists of dates and check marks under columns headed CHEVYS, MERCS, HUDSONS. What made it exciting was when something unusual came by, like a Packard, Eugene's favorite, a model called the Clipper. It had a silver captain's-wheel emblem on the hood. Eugene was always planning how someday he'd pry one off and mount it in his room. Instead he was killed by a maroon '52 Studebaker. The kind in which the front and rear look almost identical, both shaped like a chrome artillery shell—a model Eugene hated passionately.

They'd planned their Dreammobile together—the car they'd drive across-country to the Pan American Highway down to the Amazon—fins like an El Dorado's, long low hood like a Kaiser's, curves like a Jaguar's. They disagreed on whether it would have chrome spoked wheels or spinners with small blue lights.

They'd plan and wrestle on the "Boulevard," a four-foot median strip of grass separating double-lane traffic. Flat on their backs, rolling over each other between the roar of engines, the rush of tires only inches away on each side from where they struggled, gulping exhaust fumes. Of course Eugene was no match for Budhardin's greater bulk, but Budhardin would usually let him win. Eugene would wind up, flushed and panting, kneeling on Budhardin's shoulders to keep him pinned, and Budhardin would relax under the light body, turning his head in the crushed grass to watch the hubcaps spin endlessly by.

Once, when they were lying like that in the middle of five-o'clock traffic, a motorcycle jumped the median strip. The biker flew over the handlebars and before he hit they both distinctly heard him yelling, "You motherfucker!" at whoever had forced him out of his lane. Somehow he got back up, but when he took off his helmet blood was trickling out of his ears, and when he tried to talk all that came out was a reddish-pink froth. He sat down hard and slumped over, choking, and the next thing Budhardin knew, Eugene had run over and was cradling the biker's head in his lap so he could breathe. Later, walking home, Eugene started to cry because he had blood all over his jeans and he figured his old man was going to beat the shit out of him for ruining a pair of trousers.

After Eugene died somebody had drawn a circle with pink-colored chalk on the street and an arrow pointing to it with the words EUGENE'S BRAINS. Even after a season of fall rain and traffic, on his way to school he'd still been able to see the faded chalk letters on the asphalt before they finally vanished under snow.

It was getting dark now. He began to pedal. The elephant lumbered across the lot, crunching over tin cans, crashing through blowing newspaper. He turned up the alley, his shadow blotting out the shadows of the power lines against the backyard fences. He kept moving till the moon slid unbearably across his eyes in silver spots and blood rushed in waves through his head, making him too dizzy to take another step. He'd known that he was going to pass by the spot, but he hadn't expected his reaction to be this strong. It was the smell—the same smell after all these years—of rain-rotted wood, decaying leaves, catpiss fungi, of some wonderful weed the name of which he still didn't know, and behind it all the hint of damp flower beds. He stuck his trunk into the narrow Secret Gangway and inhaled.

He butted his head against the dark opening between two garages, but it was impossible for him to get any closer to the backyard on the other side. Even back then, as a child, he'd been barely able to squeeze through.

Eugene had discovered the place. He had been going there with Jennifer R., who was a grade ahead of them. Through the passage there was a yard with grass sprouting up like a wheat field around their knees. A broken birdbath stood in the middle, lopsided and dripping moss. Off to one corner, under a huge oak, was an old arbor so completely entwined with vines that the light inside was green. An old invalid lady owned the house, but her back-porch shades were always drawn and once inside the arbor, no one could see in.

They used to take turns going under Jennifer's dress. The elephant began to shudder, standing there with his trunk still in the gangway, remembering it. First the green sunlight inside the arbor and then kneeling down and entering the world of Jennifer, her legs and the way the light came through the flowered dress she wore, palms sweating, taking down her panties and *looking*.

He'd kneel there for a while and then it would be Eugene's turn and then his turn again. Once, on the way there, Eugene said, "I'm going to kiss it today." And so when it was Budhardin's turn he kissed it too. And Jennifer said, "Oh! He kissed me there!" to Eugene and Budhardin pulled his head up, feeling himself blushing, and said to Eugene, "Didn't you?" And Eugene was rolling around laughing.

Another time Eugene brought a little rubber hammer from a play-tool kit and they took turns tapping Jennifer. She seemed to like it.

The time after that Eugene asked her if she wanted to see them. At first she didn't want to but finally she did.

"We'll both show her," Eugene said. "One, two, three, pull it out!" Budhardin tried but he couldn't. He stood there frozen with guilt and embarrassment, his fly open, on the brink of damnation.

"C'mon," Eugene said, and then he reached into Budhardin's unzipped trousers and pulled out his penis. They both had boners. Jennifer started giggling. Eugene was playing with himself. He tried to get Jennifer to but she wouldn't. She was afraid of germs.

"Look, no germs," Eugene said, grabbing Budhardin's and jerking it gently.

The elephant was moaning and ramming his huge gray head into the telephone pole that stood in front of the gangway, concealing the entrance from view of the alley. Now that the dizziness had passed he was all twisted up inside and realized he couldn't just stand there anymore, he had to keep moving.

He could move off, but he couldn't stop thinking. He remembered the time they went to Ghazili's and bought balloons, then walked down the alley toward the gangway.

"What are these for?" Budhardin asked.

"You put them on your prick," Eugene said.

They practiced with a few. Budhardin struggled with a red one, stretching it over the head of his penis.

"It looks like Santa Claus," Eugene said, laughing. He had worked a yellow one partially on. "You know what I'd like to try? Sticking one of these up Jennifer and then blowing it up inside her. I wonder if she'd like that."

They were jerking each other off while talking.

"How could they have made this a mortal sin?" Budhardin said.

"A mortal sin!" Eugene looked at him, shocked. "Whataya mean a mortal sin?"

"It's against the Sixth Commandment," he said. He'd thought Eugene had realized that, that they had been sharing in a pact of mutual damnation. The closeness of damning themselves together had actually been more important than the physical pleasure.

"I wouldn't have done it if I'd of known it was a mortal sin." Eugene was looking at him as if he were weird. "You mean you knew it and still did it?"

"It's okay," Budhardin said quietly. "If you didn't know it was a mortal sin then it wasn't one."

"You sonofabitch," Eugene said—he was almost crying—"I coulda kept doing it then if you hadn't of told me!"

After Eugene went to confession he told Budhardin he'd never go to the arbor again. The priest had made him tell the whole story and for penance told him to wait until no one was looking, then to put his finger in the flame of one of the vigil candles and hold it there a moment, only a moment. And then to meditate on how eternity was a never-ending series of such moments, except the fires of hell were not one tiny flame but an inferno roaring like the bowels of a furnace.

Without Eugene, Jennifer wouldn't return either. Budhardin felt more alone than he ever had before. He could still remember in third grade, before he'd made Holy Communion, asking the priest, "If God is good how could he create something as terrible as hell?" The priest had explained that maybe hell really wasn't full of fire, that the real torture was the terrible loneliness of God withholding his love. Now he knew what that meant. Before he met Eugene he'd accepted himself as damned. From as far back as he could remember he was secretly aware of possessing a genius for understanding catechism, and it became clear to him early that he could never accept what was necessary for him to be saved. Like Lucifer, he was too proud to bow and scrape for God's love. But he hadn't grasped the extent of the pain—not until he was cut off from Eugene, could see the look of repugnance that came into his face, realized he had been cast aside as an "evil companion." He couldn't endure it, and so he decided that to win back Eugene's friendship he'd have to win his soul.

He went to Frenchie—an older, crazy guy in his twenties, who'd been in the Navy, knew every dirty joke in the world, had naked women tattooed on his ass, wore sandals, a little mustache, and a knot of beard growing out from under his lip instead of his chin. Everybody knew Frenchie was weird and avoided him. He'd come up to kids on the street, grinning as if he were their best friend, and mutter through yellow teeth, "How 'bout a little, my man?"

Frenchie traded him a pack of dirty playing cards. On one side were regular suits and numbers and on the other were photographs of people doing things together he'd never even imagined. He showed Eugene the deuce of hearts, on the other side of which was a woman smoking a cigarette with her snatch. They went together to the arbor to look at the rest.

"Look at the size of their pricks!" Eugene said. "I can hardly wait till I get older."

"Let's see if you got any bigger," Budhardin said.

That set the pattern. Without Jennifer it became more intense between the two of them. And afterward Eugene going to confession and promising Christ he wouldn't do it anymore. Father Wally warned him he was turning into a homo and urged him to pray for strength to withstand these terrible temptations. Sometimes after they did it Eugene would get sullen. Once he started to cry. But there were other times when he said he didn't care anymore, would suggest that they try something new off the cards, and Budhardin would feel a flush of joy, knowing that he had gained in his contest with Christ.

One of the times that touched him most came when

Eugene was serving mass. It was the feast of St. Lawrence, a martyr who had been grilled alive rather than deny his faith, and Eugene was wearing a white-lace surplice over a cassock, scarlet for blood. The bell rang for Communion. Father Wally turned, holding the chalice full of hosts, and stopped, as always, to give Communion to the altar boys first. They knelt before him on the plush carpeted steps leading to the altar, their eyes closed and mouths gaping in readiness (the way Eugene had knelt before Budhardin the day before). He could see Eugene's face blushing in the candlelight and the look twisting the priest's features when Eugene bowed his head, refusing to receive the host, Father Wally suddenly realizing that someone with mortal sin on his soul was helping to serve mass.

They never openly kicked Eugene out of the altar boys. He was just never asked to serve mass again. Eugene never complained, but Budhardin could see something changing within him—as if he were living in a trance, the way he slept through class with his head buried in his arms or how he walked into streets without checking traffic. That's when Budhardin conceived his plan of collecting the souls of the other boys, till there would be no one left in innocence to swing the censer or carry the heavy missal from the right side of the altar to the left during the Offertory or to mumble the Latin responses. He'd show them the cards; he'd tell them the names of the others who'd already seen them. Frenchie let him use his basement to show stag films. Budhardin took them there one by one, running the film in the dark, the light passing through cobwebs, focused on the cinder-block walls, and just at the right moment he'd stop the machine and ask them, "Would you trade your soul to see what comes next?" He already had the deeds made out, ready to sign. They always laughed when they scrawled their names in the light of a flickering candle.

The elephant gazed up. He had been traipsing down the alleys for blocks, crossing the empty streets in between, and continuing on. Now he could see the spire of the church rising over the two- and three-story roofs against a moon as pale as a pane of smoked glass. He remembered walking down the same alley in a cold drizzle and seeing the spire shrouded in fog the day of Eugene's requiem mass.

Inside the church everyone was weeping and he was never more struck by the brutality of the service, with its incredibly gruesome *Dies Irae:*

> O day of wrath! O dreadful day!
> When heaven and earth in ashes lay,
> As David and the Sibyl say.

He knew that inside the catafalque Eugene's soul was black as the black-silk vestments of the priest, black as the woolen habits of the murmuring nuns.

> What terror shall invade the mind
> When the Judge's searching eyes shall find
> And sift the deeds of all mankind!

Eugene had died in mortal sin and now while they were chanting he was burning in the fires of eternity. He wouldn't have been surprised to see the flames begin to eat through the coffin from the inside out.

> Before Thee, humbled, Lord, I lie,
> My heart like ashes, crushed and dry,
> Do Thou assist me when I die.

And finally he knew none of it was true, not hell nor heaven, nor good, nor evil, nor God, nor any trace of Eugene called a soul. Only eternity was real. And him standing in the alley in the rain. He had turned then and walked to the arbor. Jennifer was there, dressed in black and crying. He was crying too. Rain was running in rivulets through the lattice and he got down on his knees in the mud and buried his face against her, trying to burrow up her skirt. She struggled away from him, slapping his face, slipping backward. He fell on top of her and tried to open his trousers.

"It's true what they say about you," she hissed. "I hope they get you like they said."

"What?" he said. She'd stopped struggling.

"After the funeral, they're going to get you . . . all the boys. For stealing Eugene's soul."

And that evening he was awakened by a soft howling outside his window. In the yard he seemed to see figures moving. He got back in bed. He heard stones tapping against the pane. He looked out the window. In the yard he saw the figures beckoning to him, chanting, "Give us our souls."

Sometimes he'd wake and there would be a garbage-can fire just beyond the backyard fence and it would seem to him someone was in it softly screaming. No one spoke to him at school—students or nuns—it was as if he were invisible and he stopped going. One night he heard the pebbles again. He looked out the window. The yard was covered with snow. There were children below, digging a hole, a grave in his backyard, and lowering a dirt-smeared coffin into it. "Here he is," a voice said, "close to you. Give us our souls in return." The next morning he burned the deeds in an empty coffee can, scattered the ashes along dawn-empty streets, and left for what he thought would be forever.

The elephant stood before the massive church doors curling his trunk around their wrought-iron handles, but the doors were locked. He looked at the sky. It was growing lighter—not the sky itself but the expanding halos of the streetlights.

There was a side door he had used when it had been his job to ring the bells. They had given him the job because he wasn't able to be an altar boy—they couldn't find a cassock to fit him in third grade, when they picked the torchbearers, and without first being a torchbearer one could never be an altar boy. The bells were operated electrically. It was simply a matter of inserting a key at precisely the right second and switching on the bells for the correct number of rings. He'd listen to the bongs spreading out across the neighborhood and picture himself swinging from the rope, scattering pigeons, up in the steeple.

As always, the door was open. Inside, it was dim; none of the electric ceiling lights were on. Only the glow from the racks of multicolored vigil lamps and the red sanctuary light suspended above the altar. The statues stood in the niches, colored reflections flickering off their martyrs' wounds, their stigmata, their muscles knotted in spiritual exertions, their eyes stony with visions.

He dipped his trunk in the holy-water font and sucked, then quickly swooshed the water out. It was salty and stale from a thousand fingertips, with some kind of fungus floating at the bottom as in a dirty fishbowl. The tottering font crashed to the floor, shattering marble.

He shambled up the aisle toward the altar. The communion rail was closed and he tried to climb over it. The rail swayed beneath his massive weight, then collapsed in a succession of snaps like a chain of firecrackers

The altar was carefully set: vases of lilies, candles in their golden candelabra, the enormous red missal Eugene used to struggle to carry. Budhardin swept them off with one flick of his trunk, trampling them all into the carpet, then, rearing, seized hold of the base of the enormous wooden crucifix that hung over the altar, dominating the front of the church. His trunk coiled around Christ's nailed plaster feet, the blood streaming down like nail polish from hundreds of wounds above. He could feel something give and thrashed harder. High above, Christ's head shook loose, bouncing down off Budhardin's back and rolling down the altar stairs before finally coming to rest, blue eyes staring out at him from thorn-studded brows. He turned back, letting the cross take the entire weight of his body, wrenching his torso wildly back and forth till it all suddenly gave, toppling slowly like a tree, dragging the entire wall above the altar down with it.

When he came to, he was halfway down the stairs, luckily still resting on his stomach. A cloud of plaster dust hung thick like incense in the red light of the sanctuary lamp. He was surrounded by rubble, and parts of plaster and marble bodies lay strewn about him, hands still folded in prayer, broken wings, pieces of halos. Where the ornate reredos had risen above the altar was now a gaping hole, BX cables dangling through shredded lathes. The tabernacle still remained, cast iron and indestructible as a safe.

He slowly forced himself up, the broken timbers sliding off his back, and remounted the stairs to finish the job. Before the tabernacle stood the monstrance, like a gold Inca sun flaring out dagger rays, and at its center a huge empty eye, where an enormous white consecrated host—Christ's body and blood—would be inserted during Benediction. He slid the monstrance aside and parted the silken curtains that concealed the tabernacle doors.

"Dear God! What are you doing?" a voice screamed from the back of the church. An old nun came doddering up the aisle from out of the dark shadows, holding a tray of colored votive candles, probably here early to arrange the church for another day.

"What are you doing?" she shrieked.

In the gleam of candles he recognized her—Sister Eulalia, more bent and wrinkled than ever. He stood staring as if he expected her to realize who he was and start to scold. Instead the candles were clattering to the floor from her tray.

"Dear God," she kept repeating, "oh, my Christ!" Her eyeballs looked swollen behind rimless spectacles; he could see her toothless mouth gasping for breath as she began to choke, leaning against a pew and clutching at her heart. He didn't want to see her fall.

He turned back to the tabernacle, ripped the curtains away, and swung open the golden doors. The light inside seemed blinding, like radium cased in lead. He heard a cry slice through the hollows of the church, more like a war whoop than a scream, and felt a sudden weight on his back. Sister Eulalia was atop him, kicking chunks out of his hide with her sturdy nun's shoes. He tried to reach back for her with his trunk, but she gave it a twist that almost tore it off, then started lashing him across the eyeholes with the floor-length walnut-bead rosary she wore coiled around her midsection. Half blinded, he trumpeted in pain, staggering down the stairs, stumbling over the altar rail, while she lashed on, drumming with her heels and shouting curses.

He swung his body around and around in circles, trying to pitch her off, reared and bucked, but she hung with him. His body careened off the front pews and into the rack of vigil lights in front of the grotto of Our Lady. Her body was sandwiched between him and the rack. He heard her gasp and slammed her against the rack again and again until she crumpled to the floor.

He looked at her lying there among the shattered overturned candles spreading out their puddles of tallow, her black veil covering her face like a Muslim woman's, her shredded habit up around her hips, exposing her black underwear. The church was reeling. He fingered her with his trunk, pulling away what was left of the habit. She opened her eyes and looked up at him in terror.

"No, no," she screamed, "I'm a bride of Christ! I'm God's wife!"

What am I doing, he thought, has it come to this? He

plodded away, wanting only escape, down the center aisle to the front doors, but they were still locked. His head was clearing, but his ears had started to ring. To ring wildly! Then he realized it was the bells.

He hurried down the side aisle toward the doorway he'd come in. Just as he feared, Sister Eulalia had dragged her battered body to the bells and was sounding the alarm. Before he could make it to the door the rest of the nuns had swarmed into the church.

He turned from them and lumbered back down the aisle, his rump skidding as he tried to cut the corner, knocking over another rack of vigil lights. The nuns rushed after him, some of them clumping through the pews to cut him off. He galloped past the main aisle, remembering there was one more door he still might escape through—the sacristy entrance. He hurdled the broken communion rail, two nuns hanging on to his tail.

The altar boys, led by Billy Crystal, came storming out of the sacristy holding their long-pole candle extinguishers like lances. He braked and wheeled, scattering nuns, and reversed field. The church was a screaming echo chamber. The rear was in flames where he'd smashed into the virgil lights. He tried to fishtail a corner but his momentum was too much and he crashed headfirst through a confessional. His body was wedged so tight he couldn't move.

They hauled him out through the sacristy exit, still stuck in the confessional box, and set him on his side, where he lay futilely kicking his legs. He was in a little garden the nuns tended in back of the church, a rock grotto with a goldfish pond, a garden hose trickling water over the rocks. In front he could hear the sirens of fire trucks and smell the billowing smoke. All around him people were pacing and whispering, and someone was winding chains around his legs.

"The firemen want to come around back this way," a voice warned.

"No, not till we get rid of *him*."

He could hear the forklift's metal wheels grinding toward him down the flagstone path. The forks lowered and the chains were slipped over them, then the forks hoisted Budhardin, and they all began their silent procession out of the grotto and down the alley. It was just past dawn—gray light streamed through his sockets.

They marched slowly behind the jerky pace of the forklift: altar boys in one column, still holding their extinguishers, and nuns in the other, telling their beads in unison.

The alley wound behind the water-filtration plant and they left it for a huge storm drain, the forklift traveling so smoothly down the concave passageway that the procession had to jog to keep up. When they finally reemerged, the sunlight was blinding.

They stood where the drain ended in a broad lip that angled into a steep concrete runoff above the drainage canal. He could smell the acrid industrial stench of the sludge-thick water below mixed with the gentle scent of the milkweeds that sprouted in long shoots like a curtain along the bank. They were murmuring the Sign of the Cross over him and when they got to "and of the Holy Spirit" he felt them all shove together. He began to roll slowly at first, picking up velocity till he was traveling trunk over rump, the wooden confessional splintering around him and gray chunks of his body flying off, faster and faster till he bounced through the high weeds, somersaulting over the bank and landing with a resounding *bonk* in the metal bottom of a garbage scow.

He lay there stunned, as much from the fact he wasn't drowning in the quicksandlike water of the canal as from the concussion. He heard the bees he'd disturbed buzzing above him angrily in the crushed milkweed. He heard shouts and realized they had seen what had happened and were coming to finish him off. A huge hole had broken open in the elephant's side and the sky he looked out at was so blue he wanted to live just to see it. Why did they have to shout so? Lukewarm rust-stained rainwater that had gathered in the bottom of the scow was soaking through the cracks in his hide. He could see bits of mosquito larvae, suspended flecks of rust, swirls of grease. He licked it off his dry, cracked lips. The water sloshed back and forth across the bottom of the boat. A shadow passed overhead, blotting out the sun. Suddenly it struck him he was moving! He looked up into the girders and saw wheeling pigeons beneath the underside of a bridge. He could see the traffic passing overhead. The scow floated out from under, back into the sunlight. It was in the middle of the river. On each side huge glittering walls of skyscrapers loomed like canyons of glass.

He shifted so he could peer out of the eyeholes. The drop gate was partially lowered and he could see out of the front. The scow was entering the mouth of the river, passing the light tower on the delta. The water was dark brown but beyond that he could see the green horizon of the sea.

"Hey"—someone was knocking on his head—"hey, Elephant." He turned back toward the gaping hole and found himself staring into the angelic face of Billy Crystal. "Hey," Billy said, "I told them I was gonna see if you was dead, but instead I untied us and pushed off. You shoulda heard the assholes yelling. Fuck them!"

Budhardin smiled.

"Where you think we're heading," Billy Crystal said, "Europe?"

"Maybe," Budhardin said, "or maybe the Yucatán. Depends on the current."

"Well, we got rainwater to drink and garbage for bait and your tail for a line, and I can use this as a fishing pole," Billy said, shaking his extinguisher. "The only trouble is there's rats sittin' up on the bow."

"Don't worry," Budhardin said, "there's room enough for both of us in the elephant."

"South of the border!" Billy Crystal said, his choirboy mouth breaking into a grin. "Fucking A!"

The Long Thoughts

All the while he and his mother argued, the Vulcan continued to page through a beautiful leather-bound volume of Goya's etchings he'd borrowed from the Art Institute library. The dim, dirty-shaded lamplight yellowed the pages. It yellowed their whole cramped living room, turning it brown in the corners. Between the peeling wallpaper chrysanthemums and worn florals of the carpet it was one of the most depressing rooms I knew. The blinds were always drawn.

"Christ!" Vulk said. "I'd give anything to draw like that." The etching showed a bunch of human parts hacked off and hanging from a tree.

"Quit dreaming," his mother said. "Why don't you face the fact that you ain't even got the talent to pass half your regular subjects instead of trying to make your friends think you're some kind of genius? You think they believe that bullshit? They're laughing at you behind your back and getting ahead while you make a big, damn fool out of yourself."

Vulk's head fell to the side, looking too big for his short body. He opened his mouth, let his jaw gape and his tongue loll out, shaking his hair down into his face and rolling his eyes. "I am destroyed by your profundity," he said.

"I'd start to worry if I could look so convincingly retarded," his mother told him.

Vulk just sat there flipping pages and making lip farts. "You musta done something irregular when I was in the womb," he said.

"You didn't get your low IQ from me!"

"Low, my ass," he said. "It's one-forty."

"How the hell would you know what it is?"

"Because I snuck in the office and looked up my file after you scared the shit out of me with that IQ bullshit. And I don't have a distended anus either, by the way." He turned to me. "You know she used to tell me my anus was distended from sitting on the toilet so much. You must be some fuckin' nurse," he said to her.

"Your son just said *fuck* in here again," she yelled into the darkened dining room. "He's playing the big shot in front of his friends—as usual."

"Yaaah!" Vulk yelled at her. "Watch it! The Specter's looking up your dress."

His mother shot a glance over to where I sat on the floor, catching me hastily looking away as if I really had been looking up her dress. She glared at Vulk, her eyes magnified behind her white cat-framed glasses like an attacking owl's. I rolled over on my side under the coffee table trying not to laugh, remembering how their fighting used to embarrass me—now it seemed so funny it ached.

"Shit-ass," she hissed at him. "Lew, are you deaf?" she hollered. "I said Thomas is going too far in here again."

Through the legs of furniture I could see Vulk's father outlined against the space heater in the darkened dining room, watching the portable TV. The set spread its pale glow over the dirty supper dishes that surrounded it on the table. The blue flames of the space heater were reflected on the screen.

"Tom, how many times do I have to ask you not to talk to your mother like that?" His voice sounded even wearier than usual. "Take it easy on my ulcer, will you?"

Screams filtered through the hoofbeats and gunshots in the dining room. They weren't coming from the TV set. "Philip and Rosemary are fighting in the kitchen again," Vulk's father groaned. "Oh, Jesus Christ!"

"Goddammit!" his mother said, and stormed out of the room in the direction of the screaming. It got worse. We could hear Vulk's father going ooh, oooohh in the dark.

"Come in here—you gotta hear this," Vulk said. We went into his room. It was right off the front door. It must have been an entrance closet at one time but Vulk had squeezed a mattress into it. It filled the entire room and curled up at the corners. One side of it was heaped with paperbacks that almost reached the ceiling. Most of them were on psychology but there was a lot of science fiction too. On the other side a row of shelves looked ready to pull out of the plaster and bury what remained of the mattress in an avalanche of flattened paint tubes, tempera bottles, brushes, crayons, an infinite variety of stuff. The walls looked like a palette splotched and smeared with swirling rainbows, half-obscured slogans, unfinished sketches. On the ceiling he'd painted a hawklike creature wearing long underwear and a cape with a huge V for Vulcan on his chest. We sat down on each side of the record player in the sunken middle of the mattress. "Listen to this," he said. "I got it out of the library today. Shit, I didn't even know they let you take out records."

"What've they got?"

"Mostly classical."

I gave him the finger. He was on this big classical-music kick and I didn't like a lot of it.

"No, listen to this," he said. "You'll dig it."

"What is it?"

"Debussy. Piano music."

"As long as it isn't that fuckin' opera. At least turn it up."

About one A.M. his father came to the door in his underwear and asked us to turn it down. Vulk insisted that it had to be played loud or we'd miss the dynamics, so his father told us if we didn't like it to get the hell out of the house, which we did.

It was early in January and the street and trees were pale with snow. The cold seemed to intensify the quiet. Now and then a car would grind by, its snow chains jangling. We walked along past the button factory and then down the dark block past the church and grammar school we had both attended. The spire of the church threw a shadow over the street. The neighborhood didn't look so bad at night under the snow.

"Let's go see if Harry is still up," Vulk said.

We turned the corner, walking down the street I lived on. Harry lived about fifteen blocks away. He had a car that sometimes worked. It was a long walk and my ears were already beginning to feel brittle.

"Did you tell them about what happened?" I asked.

"Not yet," Vulk said, "I figure O'Donnel will call them up."

It was snowing lightly again, almost like snow being blown off the roofs and trees as we walked underneath. It didn't seem as cold when it snowed.

"What are you gonna do?"

"Shit, I don't know," he said. "Keep going to the Institute at night. Just quit, I guess. What the hell do I need a diploma for?"

We passed the apartment house I lived in. The lights were all out.

"I could probably get back into Harrison and graduate from there," Vulk said. "They never *really* kicked me out of there. I just kinda stopped going, you know . . . shit, O'Donnel still might call the cops."

"I don't think so," I said.

"You can't tell. Nobody thought they'd expel seniors either. He's crazy! When they had their inquisition this afternoon he shows the other priests all the shit he got out of my locker. First he holds up this book of nudes, so I mention I'm taking night classes at the Art Institute, then he shows them the pills, so I say they're for my old man's ulcers and must have got in there by mistake, then he starts reading passages out of some of the paperbacks in this weird tone of voice, like he's breathing real hard—it was unbelievable—I thought he was going to start beating off right there. Then he shows them this Coke bottle with a Tampax in it for a wick and I try and tell them it's an art object and Schmidt, who's supposed to be defending me, starts yelling he doesn't want it on his conscience that he defended such scum and they all agree I'm too warped to graduate from a Catholic school."

"Too warped! Jesus Christ!" I was laughing so hard I lurched over a snowbank. "Too fuckin' warped!" Our laughter came echoing back down the corridor of buildings. We cut across a block of lots where they'd knocked the buildings down, crunching over ice and rubble, stamping through dead weeds behind billboards.

I was thinking about that morning with Vulk and I as usual starting the day by kneeling on the floor in detention. We'd been there so long that I'd come to accept the fact that school would always start at seven-thirty for me. The room was full of guys slumped down sleeping, copying homework, passing around comic books, or matching for dimes. The group of us who were never able to get out of it had to kneel on the floor in front of O'Donnel's desk. We had an *esprit de corps*—everybody had a special name. Tom's was the Vulcan; mine was the Specter.

O'Donnel came in and sat behind his desk for a while staring at us. We all hung our heads, smirking into our collars and not looking him in the eye, which pissed him off. He got up from his desk and walked over to the edge of the platform it was set on, standing right before us. Then he kicked Vulk right in the stomach, his leg tossing up his cassock, his black shoe buried for a moment in Vulk's leather jacket. Vulk doubled over, then looked up and called him a sonofabitch.

"You bum! I'm going to have your ass thrown out of here today, Vukovich," O'Donnel shouted at him. "We just searched your locker and found *drugs*." Spit flew out of his lips when he talked. He looked all around the silent room, then back at Vulk. "There's a meeting in the rector's office at one regarding your expulsion. You have the right to bring a member of the faculty to defend you. Now get out."

After Vulk left, O'Donnel glared at the rest of us. "I hope you losers learn something from this," he said. "You think it's all a big joke, huh, that you're tough guys? That's how easy it is to eliminate the rotten apples. He ain't gonna find a decent job the rest of his life. He's got drugs on his record now and it'll follow him wherever he goes." He was so worked up his bald head had turned almost purple and the veins jutted out of his bulldog neck above his collar. "Some guys only learn the hard way!"

"I notice they didn't return the nudes they stole from me," Vulk said. "Maybe they're redecorating the bathroom in the monastery."

We turned down Twenty-sixth Street, walking past the boulevard, the stoplights looking pink behind the blowing snow. It was a business street and there were occasional cars passing slowly with fuzzy headlights. We passed the county jail with its dilapidated wall and blue-lit watch-towers.

"Listen to that," I said. We stopped under a streetlight, snow floating down, and faced the jail. The voice came again from one of the barred buildings beyond the wall—"Hey, you guys"—then something else we couldn't make out.

"Whataya waaaannnt?" We shouted together.

"Hey, you guys," the voice came back, but we still couldn't catch the rest of it.

We gave up and walked on. "It sounded like 'mush-rooms and sausage with anchovies' to me," I said.

"No, I think it was 'Hey, you guys, how about a little?' "

"It was goddamn spooky."

"Makes you feel really free just walkin' the streets," Vulk said. He scooped a handful of snow off the windshield of a car. "Hey, it's good packin'."

We walked the rest of the way to Harry's throwing snowballs at the streetlights.

There was nobody home. We lobbed snowballs at Harry's window for about five minutes and then climbed the rickety back stairs and shook the door. Nobody answered. We looked around outside to see if his car was there but it wasn't.

"He must have gone somewhere," Vulk said.

"No doubt about it." My gloves were soaked and my fingers frozen from throwing snowballs. My feet felt like concrete. We walked back to Twenty-sixth. The stores were gated and dimmed for the night. An occasional neon sign blinked across the sidewalk snow.

"I'm hungry," Vulk said. "Let's go sit in a restaurant."

"You got any money?"

"No. How about you?"

"Fifteen cents."

"Fifteen cents! Petit bourgeois."

"Your mama, hose nose."

He didn't say anything. I could see he was trying to think of a comeback. He was staring at the ground, his large eyes reminding me as always of a beagle's, brown and sad even when he laughed. His big nose and stocking cap made him look like one of the dwarfs. I knew he was sensitive about his nose and felt a little guilty pimping him about it when there were just the two of us. I guess he'd gone through life never being able to find the right retort.

"Just remember Cyrano," he said.

"It's probably distended from too much picking."

"Here's something distended," he said, grabbing his crotch.

"There's a meal for a working-class artist." I pointed to a gray crust of bread lying along the curb by a fire hydrant. It was surrounded by a suspicious yellow stain melted into the snow.

"You know I say disgusting things sometimes," Vulk said, "but *everything* you say is disgusting."

"You're just too warped to realize my profundity."

"No doubt about it."

We passed an all-night Laundromat, cleanly lit in white neon and empty.

"Let's sit in there awhile before I die," I said.

We went in. There was a red-lettered sign by the door that warned NO LOITERING. Vulk shook his fist at it.

"Suppose the cops come," he said.

"We'll say we were doing our laundry. I got a dirty snotrag. How about you?"

"I use my sleeve. Maybe I can wash my sleeve."

I was testing the money changers. Nothing came out. I went over to the pay phone and opened the coin-return slot. There was a dime in it.

"Eureka! Eureka!" I yelled, showing it to Vulk. He came over and examined it carefully, biting it a few times.

"Hmmm, you can always depend on the lumpenproletariat to sniff out the crumbs. Probably some blind old lady lost it."

"Maybe we can give it back." I dropped it in the phone. "Hello, hello, operator? I'd like to report finding a dime in one of your phones down here on Twenty-sixth Street. I'd like to return it to the proper party."

"You want to return a dime?"

"No doubt about it."

"Just a minute," she said. "I'll connect you with the supervisor." There was a giggle in her voice and it gave me a warm flush. I stood there holding the receiver for about a minute.

"Maybe they're tracing the call," Vulk said.

"Hello," the supervisor said.

"Yes, hello, are you there?"

"Sorry to keep you waiting—you're trying to return a dime?"

"That's right but I don't want the phone company keeping it. It says *e pluribus unum* on it if that's any aid in identification."

"All right, just hang up and we'll put it in our lost-and-found."

"Thank you." The connection was broken; the phone belched. I opened the return slot and there was the dime.

We sat down in the shining plastic contour chairs along the wall. It was a few minutes before two by the Coca-Cola clock. The Laundromat smelled of soap and bleach like a chlorinated swimming pool. The lines of washing machines gleamed. The dryers, set in the opposite wall, looked like a row of looted safes. It was nice and warm, my feet thawed and began to burn, I unzipped my jacket.

"Boy, this is the life."

"No doubt about it," Vulk said. He got up and wrung his gloves out on the floor. "Loan me your dime." He walked over to one of the dryers, stuck his gloves in, and turned it on. "A little entertainment on a frosty night."

We both sat there watching the dryer spinning around and around. I lit a cigarette. It was quiet enough to hear the wind outside through the dryer's hum, and the tiny creaks that rooms make. I put my head on my arm and closed my eyes. The heat was making me groggy. I started thinking about the homework I hadn't done. It seemed I had spent my whole life worrying about assignments I hadn't done. Suddenly more than anything I just wanted to be in bed. To get there we'd have to walk out again through the cold. It seemed stupid just sitting here; why had I let Vulk talk me into going to Harry's? Then I thought of the two of us walking down the street and him telling me that everything I said was disgusting in his most affected voice. I started laughing.

"What's so funny?" he kept asking.

I tried to tell him but every time I began, the image of the dirty crust in the snow rose up and made me laugh harder. It really was disgusting. Finally I managed to get it all out.

"What the hell's funny about that?" he coughed out. We were both holding our stomachs and crying, we were laughing so hard. "We need a fix," he said. He took out a little box of Nodoz and offered it to me. "First one's free, kid."

"If you hadn't squandered my dime we could get a couple cups of coffee."

I inserted my last dime in the coffee machine, which we kicked and beat, but still got only one cup out of it. The coffee was almost tasteless and hot. We sat there passing the steaming paper cup back and forth and popping Nodoz. I lit another cigarette. The first one was decomposing in the smeary puddles by our feet.

"Did you ever read anything by Shelley?" I asked. We'd read *Adonais* the day before in lit. class.

"I read something about his life," Vulk said. "He was pretty cool for his time, really into screwing, didn't give a shit about what the bourgeois thought."

"Like Ginsberg," I said. "No shit, when I read that poem it made me think of *Howl.*"

"Yeah, but I don't think he was a homo. Ginsberg's all around crazier. You ever read anything about van Gogh's life?"

" 'I saw the best minds of my generation destroyed by madness,' " I was reciting, listening to the Laundromat amplify it.

"That was van Gogh, all right. He really lived a weird life."

"You know reading about artists is almost as depressing as reading *The Lives of the Saints.* They all end up starving or shooting themselves or cutting their ears off. Half of them couldn't even screw without catching the syph and their dicks rotting off." I started thinking about it, totaling them up: Poe drunk in the gutter, De Quincey hooked on opium, Keats with TB, Charlie Parker, van Gogh. The Vulcan. And me showing him my poems.

"Here we go," he said. A cop walked in, his car's blue light glancing across the plate-glass window in the front.

"What are you guys doing here?"

"Just sittin'."

"Can't you read?" he said, gesturing toward the NO LOITERING sign. "Get your asses out of here."

We stood up to leave, trying to act superior. I looked at the flattened coffee cup and smashed cigarette butts lying in the puddle on the floor.

"Wait a minute," he demanded. "How old are you guys?"

"Eighteen."

"Let's see some IDs."

There was a curfew for people younger than eighteen and we both stood there searching through all our pockets like we'd lost our cards. Finally we handed them over. He stood there squinting at them, trying to compute our ages.

"Hey, you're seventeen. And you're still sixteen," he said to me. "You guys wanta wait at the station for your parents to come pick you up?"

We stood there looking belligerent, not saying anything.

"I could arrest you for loitering. What the hell are you doing here at quarter past two anyway?"

"Sitting."

"Oh, yeah?" He was still studying our names and convictlike photographs on our student-rate bus cards. "If anything's wrong we'll know where to come looking for you. Now, get home fast."

We trudged outside.

"We showed him a thing or two," Vulk said.

"Yeah."

"Why didn't you tell him your old man was Mayor Daley?"

"The prick is following us," I said. The squad car was cruising slowly behind us, its headlights dimmed. "Let's turn down the next street."

Vulk had his Chap Stick out and was smearing it on his lips.

"Oh, no," I said.

He was filling his mouth up with lighter fluid. The squad car came up even with us, the cop glaring through a half-opened window. We could hear the police calls. We stepped off the curb into the intersection. Vulk had his Zippo lighter out. He stopped in the middle of the street, turned to the squad car, and lit his lighter, spitting out an enormous yellow flame.

We took off down the side street, both yelling "*Fuck you*" at the top of our voices. I looked over my shoulder to see if the cop had turned yet. He wasn't there.

"He might be coming around the block," Vulk said. "We better turn in."

We cut down an alley, jogging through the ruts the

garbage trucks had made in the snow, our breath panting out before us. The snow was piled high against the garbage cans.

"It was funnier when I did it in Martin's class," Vulk said.

"You're really an asshole. I could see my old man getting a call at work to come get me out of jail."

The alley kept going, broken by streets. It looked like a crooked blue tunnel under the streetlights. We plodded for a while without saying anything.

"The Specter and the Vulcan floating through the night," he said.

"I'm freezing my ass off."

"Offer it up."

He stopped and I kept walking. "Wait up," he called. He was tugging a Christmas tree out of a hill of old snow, cardboard boxes full of frozen trash, and garbage bags filmed with new-fallen snow. It was a scraggly tree. Shreds of tinsel still dangled from its broken branches. We continued down the alley, Vulk dragging the tree by its tip, sweeping it behind him in the snow.

"We can warm up here," he said, "make a campfire to keep the wolves off." He lifted the tree into a trash can. We dug around and found some newspapers and garbage bags and brushed the snow off. Vulk squirted lighter fluid over everything. But even the fluid couldn't get it going. It would flare up and then be flattened by a gust of wind. The inside pages of the newspaper burned for a minute or so, but the tree wouldn't catch. We watched the paper cinders waft glowing orange out of the garbage can, black flakes with sparks at their edges flying away into the snow and dying out. Vulk was spreading his hands over the top of the can.

"Ah, nothing like a roaring hearth. Want to set a garage on fire?"

"Not tonight," I said.

After the paper burned away we gave up. The alleys seemed very dark after our staring at the flames.

"I forgot my gloves at the Laundromat," Vulk said.

"You wanta go back?"

"Hell with 'em,"

We turned off down a side street. A dog barked at us from between the slats of a fence, his mouth steaming, making the silence ring. It had never seemed as quiet—no traffic, or stalled cars groaning, or snow shovels scraping for blocks around. We came out on the boulevard and left two rows of footprints across it. Our shadows passed through the shadows of trees etched in the snow by the moonlight.

"It doesn't look too bad," I said.

"I wish I was good enough to paint it the way it is."

We came to the turnoff for my street; Vulk lived farther down.

"You going home?" he asked.

"Yeah, I guess so. You get the long thoughts tonight."

"You planned this," he said. We always calculated who'd have the longer walk home, alone with his thoughts.

"I'm really going to be beat tomorrow. I think I'll sleep during Pig's class." I didn't remember till I said it that Vulk had been expelled. "Well, I guess you get to sleep late tomorrow."

"Yeah, I guess so. I don't know. Maybe I might go down with you and just hang around, sit in Walgreen's or something."

"Okay, meet you at the bus stop."

"Yeah, so long." He turned and walked away into his thoughts.

I had the short thoughts. It was only a two-block walk past Luther Street and Washtenaw; time to wonder if Vulk was having his daydream of walking down a street in Paris and to worry again about the homework I hadn't done. Then I was before the apartment building where I lived with its dark hallway I'd been afraid of ever since I was a kid, feeling the wind blow through me, sifting up little funnels of snow off the ridges of drifts, flakes twirling in the streetlight. The street looked gentle, its soft brown slush matted white. I could feel the Nodoz making my heart pound. I could feel the spray of snow hit my face and hair, every particle, every second. I lit a cigarette, remembering the Debussy spinning over and over in Vulk's room and the two of us sitting there like madmen hunched above the record player, our eyes squeezed shut. I recalled it so clearly that for a moment I started to shake, then it slipped away, leaving me with a chill and the cigarette tasting like burned newspaper in the raw air, so I went in. My father was still working the double holiday shift at the PO and I had to clear the supper dishes from the table and wash them before going to sleep.

The Wake

Evangeline's mother had died and Jill was going to the wake. She put on her black-leather car coat even though it was a warm evening, and knotted a black-nylon scarf bandanna-style over her hair.

"Be careful what you say," her mother warned as she left the house. "You know how oversensitive Vangie is."

Jill walked down Twenty-second toward Baynor's Drugs, where she was supposed to meet Rita. They had planned to go to the wake together. The streetlights were on already though it was still light. The same old men and women she always saw on Twenty-second stood hosing their tiny squares of grass. The sidewalks smelled like rusty pipe. Jill was going to have a cherry Coke and smoke a cigarette. She'd left a little early and that's how she'd look when Rita showed up—nonchalantly sipping a drink, smoking, self-possessed, and ready for the wake. Rita was the only friend she had who could appreciate something like that. But when Jill got to Baynor's it was closed. A metal grate was padlocked over the door.

Jill waited on the step under the Rexall sign. She'd realized all along that Rita would be late as usual, but now that she had to stand on the corner it irritated her. She wanted the cigarette she'd planned on, but decided to wait till Rita got there. Even though Twenty-second was one of the big streets in the neighborhood, traffic was light. She watched it go by, listened to an airplane, thought of the people in it going somewhere.

A Pontiac pulled over, muffler rumbling low. There was a liquid promise of power in the sound, even as the car idled at the curb. Jill knew the car was hopped up and looked away so as not to seem interested. She'd vaguely noticed it circling the block—a creamy-white color with a white convertible top, glittering with chrome, the kind of car guys in the neighborhood called a Pancho. She'd caught a glimpse of the driver, a guy in a black T-shirt with greased-back blond hair, wearing silver-lensed sunglasses that shone back like mirrors. She knew he wasn't from the neighborhood. She didn't recognize the car and, besides, none of the local guys would try to pick her up like that anymore. They'd nicknamed her Frozen Custard, Miss Tastee-Freez, joked to her face about her being a vanilla sundae with a cherry on top. That's how she liked it. She wasn't going to hang around the neighborhood forever, get herself knocked up, tied down with a bunch of kids, married to a truck driver. A few of them understood that. Nobody hassled her.

"Hey," the guy inside the car was calling, "need a ride?"

Jill shook her head. She could hear the radio throbbing from inside the car, the bass turned up like at a rock concert.

"Hey, stuck-up." He laughed. "C'mon. You'll like me."

"I'm waiting for a friend," she said.

"She's not coming."

"How do you know it's a she?"

"Just know. And she's not coming."

Jill could see him flashing a smile like a model's in a suntan-lotion ad. Even his hair flashed. Suddenly she was dizzy; the car looked too white—an egg about to break. The chrome gleamed like the blade of a knife. She felt afraid. Just talking to him had been poor strategy.

She started up Twenty-second. He drove along the curb, the engine rumbling behind her, matching some vibration within her that weakened the back of her legs. When she reached the bowling alley in the middle of the block she went in.

It was air-conditioned. So cold she shivered. The lighting was mint blue. Balls thumped and gained momentum into thunder. Pins exploded at the ends of varnished lanes. She stood beside the popcorn machine. It seemed the bare light bulb the popcorn was piled under gave off heat. She dialed the pay phone next to the machine.

"Hello. Is Rita there?"

"Rita went to a wake," her mother said.

"Well, this is Jill. I was supposed to meet her at Baynor's."

"Who's this?"

"Jill. You know, Rita's friend Jill."

"Well, I don't know nothing about no Baynor's. She don't tell me nothing. You girls just do what you do and don't tell no one. So I don't know. Maybe she forgot. She's very forgetful."

"Yeah, okay, thanks." Jill hung up.

She stood in the lobby looking out the window through the blinking neon sign, picturing Rita's fat, frowsy mother. Rita had been her best friend ever since that day in fifth grade she'd shown up wearing those little hooped gold earrings. She'd had a high-school girl pierce her ears. No wonder Rita was screwed up, with a mother like that. Jill could almost smell the booze on her breath over the phone.

"They don't want you calling them alleys—they're lanes now." A woman with a beehive hairstyle giggled, pushing by Jill. The woman was talking to a guy with long sideburns, punching him in his tattooed bicep. He was grinning down at her, all the while unconsciously tugging at his crotch. It was a reflex Jill had noticed ever since high school. Like spitting. Men seemed to do it when they were unsure of themselves. She'd even seen it on TV ball games—the batter touching himself just before stepping up to the plate. The way some made the sign of the cross, Jill thought. If Rita had been there they'd both be laughing at it; without her Jill couldn't take any more of the bowling alley. Twenty-second looked empty. She stepped out.

She decided not to go back to Baynor's, that Rita had got confused and gone on to the wake. She walked toward Damen so she could stay on the main, well-lighted streets until she had to turn down Eighteenth to the funeral home. It was still light enough so that she wasn't worried. It would be dark coming home, but she'd meet Rita or someone there to walk back with.

She was passing the truck docks, the sidewalk strewn with gravel, air acrid with the smell of rubber and diesel fuel. The traffic here was usually deafening with semis, but today was Sunday. The iron bells from St. Kasimir's tolled behind her, answered by the almost musical chiming from St. Ann's, the parish she was heading for. They didn't quite agree on striking the hour. A whistle shrilled, cutting through the diffused ringing, then the pavement shook. She stood looking up as a black passenger train roared over the viaduct, windows brassy with the setting sun.

The viaduct served as a natural boundary between her neighborhood and St. Ann's. St. Ann's was an old Slavic neighborhood that had become Spanish. Jill had visited it often when she was younger, before her mother's family had all moved out to the suburbs or died. She'd played there with Evangeline as a child. Evangeline and her mother hadn't moved out. But even some of the older people who had moved insisted on being buried out of St. Ann's. Their baptismal certificates were registered there. Father Wojek, the pastor, could say the service in five languages—Latin, Polish, Ukrainian, English, and Spanish. The altar boys now were Mexican kids, their poor-looking gym shoes sticking out from black cassocks. After the service they all would get into their cars and the hearse would lead them up the old streets, past the house where the deceased had lived. Then the cortege would circle the block, passing the house one last time before setting off for the cemetery. It was the saddest part for Jill. She wondered how Evangeline, who sometimes acted half crazy already, would stand the grief the ceremony seemed designed to wring from her.

Parts of the ceremony made her skin crawl. She and Rita had once talked about the kinds of funerals they wanted. Neither of them wanted a big, old-fashioned requiem. Rita said she wanted to die young, when she was most beautiful, and have her naked body frozen in a block of crystal ice and displayed once a year on the anniversary of her death. Jill had an image of an elegant hotel, people in black tuxedos talking quietly, sipping martinis, everyone slightly regretful she had to miss the party. There was even an orchestra with violins and muted trumpets and people dancing, holding a little closer than usual. She wondered how the very rich were really buried.

As she turned down Eighteenth Street she had another image: of Evangeline leaping out of the hearse when it passed her mother's house, weeping, hair wild, those long fingernails she'd affected since childhood raking the dirt where she kneeled. Poor Vangie, Jill thought.

The houses along Eighteenth no longer looked the same. A bit shabbier. In places they'd been painted bright colors, the cheap paint already peeling off the moldy bricks. The graffiti on the fences were in Spanish. She passed the small, sunken front yards, mud-bottomed or overgrown with weeds, in either case littered with cans and bottles. At the end of the block she could see the violet neon sign of Zeijek's Funeral Home.

Zeijek's looked the same, the faded purple canopy over the entrance, the gray three-story building domed with its fake Russian onions. A few stars were out. She could hear the voices from the tavern across the street, where the men always went to drink during wakes—foreign-sounding as always.

Inside, it was dark, the lobby lit only by a desk lamp that seemed to glow green, reflecting off the blotter. She opened the book beneath it to sign her name and see if Rita's was down yet, but the pages were blank. She walked into the first parlor, past a crumbling wreath that looked set aside to be thrown away. The room was dimly lit and empty, streetlights shining in through stained-glass windows. Folding chairs had been set up, but no one was there yet.

She'd expected to find the family gathered. Friends who hadn't been seen in years. Sometimes it was just such a friend who consummated grief. She remembered when the father of a distant cousin had died, a cousin she'd once spent part of a summer with at a lake, whom she hadn't seen since. Yet, when she stood in line and walked past the casket, it was she who had moved the widow to tears. Her cousin was there too, and had merely said, "Hi." But the widow, her aunt, refused to let go of her hands, stared into her eyes, face twisting with emotion, repeating in a whisper, "Remember?"

Jill was only twelve years old at the time, but she understood what her aunt was trying to express: remember the lake, the sun, we were happy, summer as if it would never end, why must things change?

Walking away from the widow, Jill promised herself she wouldn't be trapped. She had suddenly become aware of time as something active and tangible—real as light—yet everyone around her seemed blind to it. She could actually feel its force like magnetic waves drawing her breath in and out, and realized if she could just maintain this awareness rather than fall back into the stupor of the people around her she could learn to direct her life.

But no one was here. She moved quickly through the parlor into the next room, another parlor, empty as well, and through a third, all empty, looking for Mr. Zeijek's office.

She opened a dark-varnished door into a room lit with neon, which stung her eyes after the dimness of the parlors. It looked more like a kitchen than an office, dominated by a porcelain table. The table was ribbed with grooves running down its sides. The way it slanted toward the sink made the room feel tilted. The walls were lined with glass cabinets stacked with bottles of colored fluids and neatly arranged utensils: wire, coiled tubing, an array of suction cups, needles, forceps, stainless-steel knives, an instrument that resembled a staple gun. One cabinet contained shelves of cosmetics. She opened it and smeared a fingertip of rouge on the back of her hand. This would blow Rita's mind, she thought, thinking of Rita's makeup collection, her endless sketching of mascaraed eyes. She picked up one of the smooth, shining scalpels and slipped it into her purse. She was becoming more conscious of the smell, a combination of chlorine and talcum, and suddenly started to gag. She went to the sink and turned on the taps, the smell of embalming fluid rising from the drain. She vomited and stood gasping over the sink. She felt as if she had defiled the room and she turned the water off and ran out.

The air in the viewing rooms seemed heavier with flowers. She returned to the first parlor. A new wreath stood in the doorway as if it had just been delivered. There were voices, candles had been lit, folding chairs arranged. Mourners congregated in small groups, away from the casket, heads bowed together, chatting inaudibly. Jill scanned the room for Rita. Many of the women were wearing veils. She didn't want to stare, but no one looked familiar.

A tall, balding man, smelling of after-shave, with a gold cross in his lapel, took her elbow, gently steering her toward the coffin.

"She looks beautiful. They did a wonderful job on her," he whispered.

She knelt before the bier. The casket was lined with crushed silk, its scarlet sheen hot on the heavily rouged cheeks, the carmine lips, the dyed orange hair plastic-looking as a doll's. It didn't look like a real body. They never did. Perhaps they aren't real, Jill thought, just models like store dummies, manufactured like tombstones and coffins. Rita would have liked that idea; she would have found the whole situation hilarious. Jill would have to remember to tell her, to explain that maybe no one really died at all—it was just another hoax perpetrated on children, one she was expected to accept tacitly now that she was old enough to see through it.

But, if so, they'd made a mistake on the model. She'd heard Evangeline's mother had died of cancer, wasted away to sixty pounds. This woman was voluptuous in a tawdry way, her black nightgown lacy at the bosom, plunging to reveal the swell of ample breasts.

"It's nice," the bald-headed usher whispered. He'd squeezed in on the kneeler next to Jill. "She never had them that big in life, so she asked they do something about it when they laid her out. It was her last wish." His finger stroked the curve of breasts and Jill smelled talcum again.

She quickly crossed herself and stood up, making way for the people lined behind her waiting to pay their respects. She was in the line with those waiting to offer condolences, shaking, fighting the urge to gag triggered by the smell of talcum, realizing it was more than just the smell. Her body was rebelling against her impulses—stealing the scalpel from Zeijek, standing here where she didn't belong. She knew she should leave now, go home, but she'd expected something to happen. It was a feeling that had been building ever since she'd heard Evangeline's mother had died, that some ceremony, some gesture, would jolt her life again, open her eyes to the future, revealing a direction the way her uncle's wake five years earlier had. She had disciplined her life, held herself aloof all through high school, but she was coming to feel trapped, in need of a new vision of herself.

A young man with curly blond hair and a reddish mustache looked into her face. He stood between two large wreaths, dressed in a dark-blue suit, a black armband knotted on his sleeve. He vaguely resembled the woman in the casket. There was the same voluptuous curl to his lips. His eyes were bloodshot, as if he'd been crying.

"Thank you so much for coming." His voice was automatic and flat.

"I'm very sorry," Jill said, extending her hand.

Instead of accepting it he reached for her shoulders and drew her to him, bending to kiss her cheek. "Wait for me in the lobby," he murmured as his lips brushed her ear.

She turned and walked hurriedly down the aisle. Veiled women reached out with old arms as she passed, touching her lightly, whispering, "Good to see you, dear."

The lobby was still dark. She leaned against the wall, trying to steady herself, and lit the cigarette she'd been saving since early evening when Rita hadn't shown. It seemed so much longer than an hour ago, standing before Baynor's in the twilight watching traffic. She'd seen something in his blue eyes more important than grief. She wanted him to show her what that was. Better not to think about it till he's here, she told herself. But when she closed her eyes she could feel his hands on her shoulders again, slipping down her arms, drawing her against him. Hurry, she thought, grinding the cigarette out on the tiled floor.

"What are you doing here?" a woman's voice demanded, echoing from the alcove where the coats were hung.

There was a pitch of hysteria to it and for a moment Jill thought it was Evangeline.

The woman stepped out. Even in the shadows Jill could see how heavily made-up she was, like the corpse's twin, her eyes orchids of eye shadow. "I saw you butting in on my poor sister's boy."

"I'm very sorry about your sister," Jill said.

"Sorry about my sister? How could you be sorry?" She stepped closer, eyes wild-looking, mascara streaked down her cheeks. She was speaking too loud. Jill glanced toward the parlor. People were looking out. The woman pointed at Jill. "Who invited her?"

"I thought she was someone else," Jill whispered.

"Someone else? She's *dead!* Oh, God! You bitch! Get her out of here," she began to scream. "Get her out!"

The mourners from the next room crowded about the doorway, staring out, shocked, muttering among themselves. Jill could hear the bald-headed man repeating, "I thought you knew her," to the women raising their veils for a better look. She could see the blond young man left alone by the casket, kneeling, his face buried in his hands, weeping bitterly.

"It should be you in the casket," Jill said to the woman, and rushed out the door.

The street was dark. Zeijek's violet neon sign was out.

She leaned dizzily against the brick wall, hoping she wouldn't be sick again. *Salsa*, sensual and rhythmic, filtered out of the little bar across the street, light from its sign red on the sidewalk. For a moment she had an impulse to enter the bar and dance, to abandon herself to the music as if it were natural for her to do so, as if she'd lived in this neighborhood all her life and everyone knew her. But to the men in the bar she would be the ultimate stranger; even as she thought about it she knew she wouldn't go in.

Instead she started back up Eighteenth Street. Windows were open, airing smells of cornmeal and frying oil, radios tuned to Latin stations, voices that stopped suddenly as she passed. She could feel eyes following her from doorways and walked as quickly as possible without breaking into a run along the outer edge of the sidewalk.

A gang of kids sitting on the steps across the street crossed over. She could hear them laughing, voices high and excited like eighth-graders', leather heels clumping behind her in the clumsy gait of adolescence. This was the poorest block, the mud in the sunken front yards smelling of urine and wine.

"Buy a flower?" a delicate child asked, stepping out of a gangway with a cardboard box full of crude paper roses.

Jill kept walking, the little girl with flowers keeping pace beside her.

"Here," Jill said, fishing out a quarter and accepting a flower.

"Flower is a dollar," the girl said, still smiling.

"Sorry, I don't have it." Jill tried to give the rose back, but the girl wouldn't take it. Instead she dropped back a few steps, repeating, "Flower is a dollar. A dollar."

"Hey," one of the guys from the gang behind yelled, "pay the kid!"

She could hear them clumping faster to catch up, swearing and joking, and kept walking. There was a lighted cart down at the next corner she recognized as the Hot-Tamale Man's. He came to her neighborhood too, had been coming since she could remember, making summer nights special with his little cart twinkling with Christmas-tree bulbs, steaming with hot tamales and red-hots. She kept herself from breaking into a run. They wouldn't try anything with him standing there. She could see the Hot-Tamale Man under his striped umbrella with its fringe of winking lights, his face expressionless as he watched her approach. A hand grabbed her jacket from behind and she pulled away.

"Would you help me?" she said, ten feet away, trying to sound calm, realizing she'd never said anything to him before except what she wanted on her hotdog, never heard him speak.

He stared down at the slice of onion he was chopping with a paring knife as if he hadn't heard her.

"Could I just stand here with you?" she asked.

Maybe he couldn't hear.

"Nobody's hurting you," one of the gang said.

"Please," she whispered.

The Tamale Man opened both compartments of his cart and clouds of steam vapored about them. She stepped into the steam as if it could hide her, pressing against the cart in its ring of colored lights. The Tamale Man was poking buns into the compartments with his forceps, snapping them like a claw, then he slammed the covers down and the steam began to vanish. She could see the gang surrounding them. He began to push the cart past her, moving in the direction she'd just come from, the cart hissing, his forceps still clacking. The gang opened to let the cart through, then closed. She watched it roll away, trailing a smell like childhood—wisps of steamed hotdogs and onions.

"Flower is a dollar," the little girl said.

One of the guys lunged, catching her purse by the

strap, but the strap was half worn through already and it snapped off in his hand, leaving Jill still clutching the bag. The rest of them broke up laughing, but the kid left holding the strap whipped it twice across the back of her legs. She could see the high, hard heels on their boots and remembered guys in her neighborhood warning one another never to go down if they got jumped because getting stomped with those heels cut you to shreds.

"What you doin' around here?"

"I was at a wake. Please," Jill pleaded, "my mother died."

"That's bullshit, man! I can see it in your eyes. You hear this bitch lying about her own mother?"

The Pancho screeched, swinging a U in the middle of Eigthteenth, swerved next to her, revving along the curb, the same car she'd seen earlier at Baynor's. The gang stood staring at it.

"Don't just stand there, babe, get in!" the driver called over the roaring pipes.

They were cruising down the boulevard, past the lighted contagious-disease hospital on Thirty-first, up the ramp onto the expressway, under reflecting green signs on overpasses that read INDIANA. The Pancho weaved through traffic, passing with a *whump*, radio blaring. Jill sat back breathing hard, opening her eyes at intervals to see where they were, not sure if she was trying to cry or trying not to.

"Here." Rita smiled, taking a joint from between the driver's lips, holding it for Jill as she inhaled.

"Relax, babe, enjoy the ride. You're with a class driver," the blond guy said.

Rita laughed. She was sitting in the middle, between Jill and the driver. Except for a "hi," she'd hardly said anything, acting almost as if Jill had intruded. She took the joint back, sucked in deeply herself, then leaned across the steering wheel to blow smoke from her mouth into his. They'd been making out on and off like that ever since Jill had jumped in. She watched Rita's lilac-painted fingernails raking through his greasy blond hair while her other hand, joint still fuming between her dime-store rings, teased toward his groin along the inside of his thigh. The car drifted across two lanes, scraping the guardrail before he whipped the wheel back.

"Let *me* drive," Rita said.

"Drive my car?"

"Yeah," Rita said, "that way you can sit next to both of us."

Jill stared at both of them in the light of the dashboard. She suddenly had the dizzying thought that Rita, her best friend, was setting her up. But Rita's face was cool as usual under a mask of makeup, giving nothing away. The driver was still wearing his silver-lensed aviator shades. His black T-shirt stretched tight over his muscles and part of a skull tattoo was showing high on his bicep where a pack of Kools was rolled in the sleeve. He caught her staring, grinned, then rolled the window down and spit. Wind and engine roared through the car, garbling music, swirling their hair. Jill's scarf blew into her face and she retied it around her throat.

He seemed oblivious of the rushing air, lounged against the open window, one hand nonchalantly playing the top of the wheel, drumming in time to what sounded like pure static. She wondered if he was on some heavier drug.

"Come on," Rita said.

"Okay, but you go where I tell you." He boosted up in the seat, stomping the accelerator. Jill watched the speedometer jitter over 120 as Rita slid under him, taking the wheel.

"Nice flower," he said, settling beside Jill. She hadn't realized she was still holding it.

"This might sound weird," Jill said, "but I went to the wrong wake."

"What's weird about that? They're all the wrong one. Hey, honey," he said to Rita, "turn at the next exit. I know a great drive-in movie way out in the sticks." He'd thrown his arms around their shoulders, hugging them all close together.

Jill watched the exit sign looming toward them on the right, but Rita didn't turn.

"Have a ball tonight," the driver was singing, along with the crackling radio, in a fake hillbilly twang.

"I used to only drive motorcycles," he whispered to Jill as if confiding a secret, "but cycles ain't got music. Don't music make everything all right?" He darted his tongue in her ear.

She turned her head to kiss him but caught a glimpse of herself, tiny and distorted, in the lenses of his sunglasses just before closing her eyes. She could see the young man she'd waited for at the wake so clearly in her mind, standing elegant and sad between those wreaths with something in his blue eyes more important than grief. The driver was trying to pry his tongue between her lips so desperately that she could feel its spongy pores. She pushed back in a hard kiss but wouldn't open her mouth.

"You know, the biggest sin is not living when you got the chance," he said.

"The biggest sin is taking away someone's chance," Rita answered.

"You missed the turnoff," he told her. "You girls don't like the movies, then I'm gonna take you to the ugliest place in the world. After that everything will look beautiful—even your crummy neighborhood."

He grabbed the steering wheel and the car squealed, fishtailing up an exit marked GARY in iridescent letters. The momentum shoved them all closer together and he yanked their jackets back off their shoulders, each of his hands then cupping a breast.

"Both got leather jackets. It's like I got two leather wings."

Jill could see the windows flashing like acetylene as they sped past foundries and refineries, the sky lit up with the coke aura of blast furnaces, towering smokestacks rimmed with red beacons erupting flame, and the air choking with carbon and smoldering rubber the way it smelled at stock-car races.

He'd worked Rita's sweater up and when the buttons wouldn't come undone on Jill's blouse he jerked them open.

"Yours are bigger," he said to Rita, "but she's got pear-shaped."

"You motherfucker," Jill said, "you dirty bastard, you prick, you cocksucker, fucking sonofabitch." The words were ripping out of her mouth, cutting through radio static before being blurred away by wind, every obscenity she could remember hearing on the street, reading on walls, whispered in jokes. She reached in her purse for a Kleenex and smeared her tears. When she stuffed the Kleenex back she felt for the scalpel. Her fingers had gone numb. She was holding something in her fist but couldn't tell if it was the scalpel or a ball pen.

"Can't have beauty without ugliness," he was saying.

"Who needs this?" Rita asked her, then suddenly spun the wheel and hit the brake. They skidded off the road along the soft shoulder, gravel *ping*ing up over the hood. Jill's neck whipped as the car swerved, the driver's glasses making an eggshell crunch as his head smacked the windshield. As soon as they rocked to a stop Jill was out her door, running through the smoke surrounding the car, afraid it would explode. She scrambled up the incline and back onto the highway, then turned to look for Rita.

Smoke was settling on the red brake lights, the Pancho dug into the edge of a ditch, one headlight beaming up through the weeds. Rita was still inside, but the driver was stumbling out, the heel of his hand pressed to his nostrils.

She ran farther down the highway, then turned again. He was standing on the road. In the dark he didn't look as rangy as she'd thought. His legs were short; his jeans hung lopsided on his hips. There was something vulnerable about him outside the car, like a creature that had lost its shell, his deadly energy drained. They stood staring at each other, listening to Rita gunning the engine and the wheels spinning in the ditch, as if whatever would happen depended on that. When the Pancho dug out in reverse, jolted gears, and bumped forward onto the highway, he shrugged at Jill as if saying good-bye and turned back to the car. It was coasting away slowly and he had to jog to catch up.

"Hold it," he called, but the car kept rolling. He tried to grab the door but couldn't hang on. He was running alongside, pounding the fender with his fist, cursing and pleading, sounding breathless as the car picked up speed and he ran harder.

Jill watched the taillights shrink, leaving the highway darker and darker. She crossed the grassy median strip and started walking along the gravel shoulder in the opposite direction, toward the dull-red glow in the sky she knew must be Gary. She imagined she could still hear him shouting each time the wind blew, voice pitched high with anger and pain. He was just another kid, she thought, and for some reason the thought startled her. She had a vision of the boy at the wake, kneeling alone, weeping into his hands, and then of all the boys in their leather jackets on the corners, in doorways, hiding their faces and weeping as if they'd lost something very dear to them they could never get back.

Lightning throbbed in a night sky that was more maroon than black and she wasn't sure if it was lightning or a discharge from the steel mills. A single headlight was gaining on her down the highway. She kept walking till the Pancho, one headlight broken, pulled alongside.

"All ours." Rita smiled as Jill got in. "Nice, huh?"

"Nice," Jill said.

"We can go anywhere."

"Well, where to?"

By the time they got back to the neighborhood it was raining. The windows were rolled up and steam gathered inside like fog. Drops flattened and rolled across the windshield, absorbing passing headlights. Rita flicked the wipers on and drove slower. Traffic followed in a long, careful line. They cruised down Twenty-second.

"Look," Rita said, "Sultana's Beauty Salon!"

Its indigo neon sign glowed behind a padlocked accordion gate.

"There's Leader's Department Store," Jill said. "I used to be afraid of its revolving door."

"Dressel's Bakery, Swanson's Dresses."

"Baynor's!"

Rita turned, driving down side streets, up alleys. Nobody was standing in the doorways. Rain slashed through streetlights on empty corners.

"I wonder if they're all tuned to the same station we are," Rita said, glancing at the column of headlights in the rearview mirror.

They turned down Jill's block, slowing to a crawl as they passed her darkened apartment building.

"Let's go by yours too," Jill said.

"You know, he was right about music," Rita said. "With the radio playing everything seems all right. I wish I could hear it every minute of my life like they do in movies. I wonder if they could wire a person's brain for that. That's how I'd like to die—listening to music high, driving around at night."

Jill didn't answer. She felt if she could see the people in the line of cars behind them they'd be everyone she'd ever known. She'd gone to the wake, and now she could see what Rita was really talking about—it was only your own death that showed how life should be lived. She listened to the music, the electric guitar reaching for the upper, aching registers, a song about an angel, as her house went by again and again.

Sauerkraut Soup

I couldn't eat. Puking felt like crying. At first, I almost enjoyed it the way people do who say they had a good cry. I had a good puke or two. But I was getting tired of sleeping in a crouch.

"It's not cancer; it's not even flu," the doctor told me.

"What is it?"

"Are you nervous?"

"Puking makes me nervous."

"It's not nerves. It's lack of nerve," Harry, my best friend, a psych major, told me.

He'd come over to try exorcising it—whatever *it* was—with a gallon of Pisano. Like all *its*, it swam in the subconscious, that flooded sewer pipe phosphorescent with jellyfish. We believed in drink the way saints believed in angels.

It took till four in the morning to kill the Pisano, listening to Harry's current favorites, the "Moonlight

Sonata" and "Ghost Trio," over and over on the little Admiral stereo with speakers unfolded like wings. We were composing a letter to a girl Harry had met at a parapsychology convention. All he'd say about her is that she lived in Ohio and had told him, "Ectoplasm is the come of the dead."

He opened the letter: "In your hair the midnight hovers . . . ."

"Take 'the' out, at least," I said.

"Why? It sounds more poetic."

"It's melodramatic."

"She's from Ohio, man. She craves melodrama."

Working on that theory, we wrote he was alone, listening to the "Moonlight Sonata," sipping wine, waiting for dawn, thinking of her far away across the prairie in Ohio, thinking of the moonlight entering her bedroom window and stealing across her body, her breasts, her thighs. We ended with the line "My dick is a moonbeam."

I watched him lick the envelope and suddenly my mouth seemed full of glue and the taste of stamps. My tongue was pasted to the roof of my mouth. I gagged. From dawn till noon I heaved up wine while Harry lay passed out on the floor, the needle clicking at the end of the record. It felt like weeping.

After a week's hunger strike against myself I still didn't know what I was protesting. Nothing like this had ever happened to me before. I did remember my father telling me he'd had an ulcer in his twenties. It was during the war. He'd just been married and was trying to get his high-school diploma in night school, working at a factory all day. Once, climbing the stairs to the El, the pain hit him so hard he doubled up and couldn't make it to the platform. He sat on the stairs groaning, listening to the trains roar overhead while rush-hour crowds shoved by him. Nobody tried to help.

"Must have figured me for a drunk," he said.

It was one of his few good stories, the only one except for the time he'd ridden a freight to Montana during the Depression, when I could imagine him young.

You're getting melodramatic, I told myself. I had begun lecturing myself, addressing myself by name. Take it easy, Frank, old boy. I would have rather said, Tony, old boy. Tony was my middle name, after a favorite uncle, a war hero at nineteen, shot up during a high-altitude bombing mission over Germany. He'd returned from the war half deaf and crazy. He'd perfected a whistle as piercing as a siren and all he did for three years was whistle and drink. He had hooded, melancholy eyes like Robert Mitchum's. His name was Anthony, but everybody called him Casey. Franklin is a name I'd never especially liked. My father said he'd given it to me because it sounded like a good business name. I'd never been successful in getting people to call me Tony. You're a Frankie, not a Tony, they'd say. Finally, I regressed to what they'd called me in the neighborhood: Marzek. Nobody used first names there, where every last name could be spit out like an insult. There was no melodrama in a last name. People are starving in this world, Marzek, and you aren't eating. Famine. War. Madness. What right do you have to suffer? Trying to hold your guts together on the Western Avenue bus riding to work. At your age Casey was taking flak over Germany.

I worked part time for an ice-cream company on Forty-seventh. Supposedly, I was going to school during the day and so I didn't get to the factory till after three, when the lines were already shut down. It was October. The lines that ran overtime in summer shut down early in fall.

A few of the production crew were usually still around, the ones who'd gotten too sticky to go home without showering, and the Greeks who'd worked in the freezers since seven A.M. still trying to thaw dry ice from their lungs and marrow. The locker room stank of piled coveralls marinating in sweat, sour milk, and the sweet ingredients of ice cream. I opened my locker and unhooked my coveralls from the handle of the push broom. That terrible lack of sympathy pervading all locker rooms hung in the air.

"Look how awful he looks," Nick said to Yorgo. "Skin and bones."

I quickly tugged on my coveralls.

"Moves like he got a popsicle up the ass," Yorgo said.

"It's a fudgsicle. Greek cure for hemorrhoids."

"He got morning sickness," Nick said.

"It's punishment for being a smartass. God is punishing you. You think you don't pay sooner or later," Yorgo said.

"I'm paying."

"You only *think* you're paying. Just wait. You won't believe how much more expensive it gets."

I pushed my broom along the darkened corridors, a dune of dust and green floor-cleaning compound forming before me. The floor compound reminded me of nuns. They'd sprinkle it on vomit whenever someone got sick in class. Vomit filled my thoughts and memories.

Has it come to this, Marzek?

It's what Harry had kept mumbling as I barfed up Pisano. It was his favorite expression. *Has it come to this,* he'd ask at the subway window as he paid his fare, at restaurants when they brought the check, at the end of the first movement of the "Moonlight Sonata," in letters to Ohio.

A month ago it had been summer. I'd worked production, overtime till six P.M., saving money for school. At night I'd played softball—shortstop for a team called the Jokers. I hadn't played softball since early in high school. This was different, the city softball league. Most of the guys were older, playing after work. The park was crowded with girlfriends, wives, and kids. They spread beach blankets behind the backstop, grilled hotdogs, set out potato salad, jugs of lemonade. Sometimes, in a tight game with runners on, digging in at short, ready to break with the ball, a peace I'd never felt before would paralyze the diamond. For a moment of eternal stillness I felt as if I were cocked at the very heart of the Midwest.

We played for keggers and after the game, chaperoned by the black guys on the team, we made the rounds of the blues bars on the South Side, still wearing our black-and-gold-satin Joker jerseys. We ate slabs of barbecued ribs with slaw from smoky little storefront rib houses or stopped at takeout places along the river for shrimp. Life at its most ordinary seemed rich with possibility.

In September we played for the division championship and lost 10–9. Afterward there was a party that went on all night. We hugged and laughed and replayed the season. Two of the wives stripped their blouses off and danced in bras. The first baseman got into a fist fight with the left fielder.

When I woke hung over it was Monday. I knew I'd never see any Jokers again. I lay in bed feeling more guilty than free about not going to work. I'd worked full time all summer and had decided to take the last week off before school began. I wanted to do nothing but lie around for a solid week. My tiny apartment was crammed with books I'd been wanting to read and wouldn't have a chance to read once school started. I'd been reading Russians all summer and wanted now to concentrate on Dostoevsky.

"Anybody who spells his name so many different ways has got to be great," Harry said.

I started with *Notes from the Underground*, then read *The Possessed* and *The Idiot*. The night before school reopened I read *Crime and Punishment* in a single sitting. It was early in the morning when I closed the book, went straight to the bathroom, and threw up. That was the first time it felt like crying.

In high school the priests had cautioned us about the danger of books.

"The wrong ones will warp your mind more than it is already, Marzek."

I tried to find out what the wrong ones were so I could read them. I had already developed my basic principle of Catholic education—the Double Reverse: *(1) suspect what they teach you; (2) study what they condemn.*

My father had inadvertently helped lay the foundation of the Double Reverse. Like the priests, he'd tried to save me.

"Math," he'd say. "Learn your tables. Learn square roots!"

On Christmas and birthdays he'd shower me with slide rules, T squares, drafting kits, erector sets. Each Sunday he pored over the want ads while I read the comics. He was resigned to his job at the factory, but he was looking for jobs for me—following trends, guiding my life by the help-wanteds the way some parents relied on Dr. Spock. By the time I was in sixth grade he'd begun keeping tally sheets, statistics, plotting graphs.

"Engineers! They are always looking for engineers—electrical engineers, chemical engineers, mechanical engineers."

It was what he'd wanted to be, but he'd never had the chance to go to college.

I enrolled in drafting class, machine shop, wood shop, math. When I became the first person in the history of Holy Angels High to fail wood shop without even completing the first project, a sanding block, he became seriously concerned.

"You gotta be more practical. Get your mind on what's real. I used to read Nick Carter mysteries all the time when I was a kid. I read hundreds. Then, one day I asked myself, Is this practical or just another way they make a sucker out of you? Who's it helping? Me or Nick Carter? I never read another."

"But Shakespeare," I said.

"Shakespeare? Don't you see that one well-designed bridge is worth more than everything Shakespeare ever wrote?"

I swept my broom past the lunchroom. I thought about my first day working the production line. When they relieved me I got my lunch, thinking it was noon. It was only the ten-fifteen break. Sweeping floors seemed like relaxation after production. But people endured the line year after year. Except in Dostoevsky's novels I couldn't think of having ever met anyone purified by suffering. I didn't want Siberia. The freezers were bad enough. People were condemned to them every day—without plotting against the czar.

The cleanup shift was in the lunchroom taking one of several breaks. The men worked after the bosses had gone and were pretty much on their own so long as the machines were clean in the morning. Unlike for the production crew, a break for cleanup didn't mean a ten-cent machine coffee. It meant feasting. Most of them were Slavs, missing parts of hands and arms that had been chewed off while trying to clean machines that hadn't been properly disconnected. I could never exactly identify where in Eastern Europe any of them were from.

"Russian?" I'd ask.

No, no—vigorous denial.

"Polish?"

No. They'd smile, shaking their heads in amusement.

"Lithuanian?"

Ho, ho, ho. Much laughter and poking one another.

"Bohemian?"

Stunned amazement that I could suggest such a thing.

The lunch table was spread as for a buffet. Swollen gray sausages steaming garlic, raw onions, dark bread, horse-radish, fish roe.

Still, despite the banquet, a sullen, suspicious air pervaded the room. Next to the cleanup crew, the Greeks from the freezer were cheerful. Not that they weren't always friendly toward me, though they were distressed that I was sweeping floors, as that had previously been "a colored's job."

"Want *y'et?*" the burly, red-bearded man missing the index fingers of both hands asked, offering rye bread spread with pigs' brains from the communal can.

Cleanup always offered me food, urging *y'et, y'et.* It rhymed with *nyet*, but I suspected it was one of those foreign words actually manufactured out of English—some contraction of "you" and "eat." They'd been concerned with my eating habits since the time they'd seen me plunge my arm up to the elbow into the whey and scoop out a handful of feta cheese from the barrel the Greeks kept in the fruit cooler.

"*Nyet, nyet,*" they'd groaned then, screwing up their faces in disgust.

"*Nyet, nyet,*" I said apologetically now, declining the brains, pointing to my stomach and miming the heaves. "Can't eat . . . sick . . . stomach . . ." I explained, lapsing into broken English as if they'd understand me better.

"Have to *y'et.* No *y'et*, no live."

"That's true."

"*Y'et* ice cream? Dixie cup? Creamsicle?"

"*Y'et* ice cream!" The idea startled me. After a summer of production, ice cream seemed no more edible than machinery. I wanted to sit down at this cleanup banquet table and discuss it. To find out how it had remained food for them; what it was like to work in after-hours America. They knew something they were hiding. I wanted to explore paradox with them: how was vomiting the same as crying? Dostoevsky like softball? Were factory wounds different from war wounds? We could discuss ice cream. How did working transmute it from that delight of childhood into a product as appetizing as lead? But my broom seemed to be drawing me away as if on gliders, down unswept, dark, waxed corridors.

Besides, the engineering of ice cream is another problem. This is about soup. Or *zupa*, as cleanup called it. They called it after me, the words echoing down the corridor like their final pronouncement as I glided away: *y'et zupa . . . zupa . . . zupa . . .*

I stood before my locker stripping off my coveralls, gagging on the sweaty-sweet effluvia of flavors hovering around the laundry bin—strawberry, burgundy cherry, black walnut, butter brickle. *Zupa*—chicken broth, beef barley, cream of celery—sounded like an antidote, the way black olives and goat cheese could counterbalance a morning of working with chocolate marshmallow, or pigs' brains on rye neutralize tutti-frutti.

It was six when I punched out; the deceptive light of Indian summer was still pink on the sidewalks. I walked, paycheck in my pocket, along the grassy median of Western Boulevard, traffic whizzing on both sides like sliding, computerized walls of metal and glass. Workers were racing away from the factories that lined Western, down streets that resembled nothing so much as production lines, returning to resume real lives, trailing the dreams they survived by like exhaust fumes–promotions, lotteries, jackpots, daily doubles, sex, being discovered by Hollywood, by New York, by Nashville, sex, going back to school, going into real estate, stocks, patents, sex, embezzlements, extortions, hijackings, kidnappings, wills of distant millionaire uncles, sex . . .

These were things we'd talked about all summer while the ice cream filed by. Now I was free of it, weaving slightly as I followed the wavy trails of strawlike cuttings the mowers had left. I could still feel the envy I'd had all summer for the guys riding the mowers over the boulevards, shirts off, tanning, ogling sunbathing girls while grass tossed through the almost musical rotary blades. It had seemed like freedom next to working in a factory, but those were city jobs and you had to know somebody to get one.

The factory had changed my way of thinking more in one summer than my entire education had. Beneath the *who-gives-a-shit* attitude there was something serious about it I couldn't articulate even to myself, something everyone seemed to accept, to take for granted, finally to ignore. It had to do with the way time was surrendered—I knew that, and also knew it was what my father, who'd worked in a factory all his life, had wanted to tell me. But he'd never been able to find the words either, had never heard them or read them anywhere, and so distrusted language.

My stomach was knotted. I was feeling dizzy and for a moment thought it might be because the line of grass cuttings I was following was crooked. When I stood still the colors of the trees looked ready to fly apart like the points of unmixed pigment in the van Gogh self-portrait I'd stare at every time I went to the Art Institute trying to provoke that very sensation. It wasn't a sensation I wanted to be feeling now. I sat down in the grass and lowered my head, trying to clear the spots from my eyes. I tried breathing rhythmically, looking away from the trees to the buildings across the street. The flaring light slanted orange along the brick walls in a way that made them appear two-dimensional, faked. The sky looked phony too, flat clouds like cutouts pasted on rather than floating. It looked possible to reach up and touch the sky, and poke a finger through.

I was starting to go nuts. It was one of those moments when the ordinariness is suddenly stripped away and you feel yourself teetering between futures. Then, at a restaurant across the street, under a Coca-Cola sign, I ate a bowl of soup and was reprieved.

A week later I doubt if I thought much about any of it—the weepy, wrenching heaves that felt like spitting out the name Raskolnikov, the involuntary fast, the universe turning to tissue on Western Boulevard. It was a near-miss and near-misses are easy to forget if we notice them at all. In America one takes a charmed life for granted.

Casey once told me that's what had seemed strange to him when he first got back from the war. People seemed unaware they were about to die. It took him the next three years of whistling like a siren to readjust. By then he'd drunk himself into an enlarged liver, having settled back into the old neighborhood, where the railroad viaduct separated the houses from the factories and every corner was a tavern. His entire life had become a near-miss at nineteen.

When I try to recall the times I almost died I get bogged down in childhood—repeated incidents like Swantek (who at age twelve was more psychotic than any other person I've ever met) demonstrating a new switchblade by flinging it at my head, grazing an ear as it twanged into a door. But my closest call would come a few years after that day I opted for *zupa* on Western Boulevard. It was as Casey had observed—I had no awareness of death at the time, though certainly there were strong hints.

By then the ice-cream factory was only a memory. I'd finished college and was working for the Cook County Department of Public Aid on the South Side. I was living on the North Side in an efficiency apartment half a block from the lake. It was August, hot, and for the last few days there'd been a faint, sweetly putrid smell around the refrigerator. For the first time since I'd lived there I stripped the shelves and scrubbed everything with Kitchen Klenzer. While I was at it I even cleaned under the burners on the stove.

The smell only got stronger, except now it was tinged with bleach. I tried moving the refrigerator, but it was one of those types in a recess in the wall and I couldn't budge it.

I went downstairs and rang the manager's bell. No answer. By the time I got back to my apartment the smell had permeated the entire room. I got a towel and blanket and left to sleep the night out on the beach.

As soon as I hit the street I knew something was wrong. Police and ambulance flashers whirled blue and scarlet at the end of the block, fusing into a violet throb. Shadows hurried away from the beach in the dark, cutting across lawns where sprinklers whipped under streetlights. At the end of the sidewalk a couple of cops had a kid pinned down, his face grinding in sand, eyes rolling as if he were having a fit. Flashlights moved slowly across the dark beach and groans and crying echoed over the hollow lapping of water. I hung around long enough to find out what had happened. A local gang, ripped on drugs, had made a lightning raid with bats, knives, and chains. Apparently they were after a rival gang, but anyone out on the beach had been attacked.

Back in my apartment I smoked an old cigar, trying to smother the smell long enough to fall asleep. I was still tossing, half awake, sweating, trying to suck breath through a cold towel without smelling, when the buzzer rang around two A.M. It was Harry with a fifth of old Guckenheimer.

"What the hell's the stench in here?" he asked.

"BO?"

"No." He sniffed. "I know that smell. It's death! Yeah, death, all right—rotting, decomposing flesh . . . decay, rot, putrescence . . . maggots, worms . . . that's it, all right, the real stuff. Where'd you hide the body?"

"Behind the fridge."

"Don't worry. You can cop an insanity plea. I'll get you a nice wing. Something quiet with the seniles—take a lot of naps. No, it gets too petty there. Maybe the hydrocephalics. You'd have to drink a lot more water to fit in. Aaaiiiyyyeee!" he suddenly screamed. "See them? There! Giant, swollen heads!" He was pointing at the window, eyes wild. "Whiskey, I need whiskey," he rasped, slugging from the bottle, then wiping his mouth with the back of his hand. "Aaaiiiyyyeee." He shuddered quietly.

Aaaiiiyyyeee had replaced *Has it come to this* in his lexicon since he'd been working at Dunning, the state mental hospital. He claimed to see hydrocephalics everywhere.

We walked out along the cooling streets, away from the lake, into a deserted neighborhood where blue neon Stars of David glowed behind grated shop windows. We were passing the old Guckenheimer, washing it down at water fountains, trading stories on our usual subjects—poverty, madness, slums, asylums—laughing like crazy. Harry kept breaking into the childhood song he'd started singing in my apartment:

> "*The worms crawl in,*
> *The worms crawl out,*
> *They turn your guts*
> *To sauerkraut. . . .* "

About four in the morning we found an open liquor store and bought another bottle. We sat drinking on a bench on the Howard Street El platform. Howard was the end of the line. El cars were stacked on the tracks, paralyzed, darkened, in lines that crossed the border into Evanston.

"We could probably walk to the next station before the train comes," Harry said.

We jumped down on the tracks and started walking, stepping carefully along the ties. The tracks looked down on the streetlights. We were even with roofs and windows reflecting moonlight. It was lovely, but we kept checking behind us for the single headlight that meant the train was coming. Then we'd have to jump the electric rail to the next set of tracks. The only danger was if we caught trains coming in both directions. We weren't saying much, our ears straining to hear the distant roar of the El, but it was perfectly still.

"This is the feeling I sometimes get in flying dreams," I said.

It was in that mood of ecstasy that I decided to piss on the third rail. It suddenly seemed like something I'd always wanted to do. I straddled it carefully and unzipped my fly. I was just ready to let go when Harry split the silence with an *Aaaiiiyyyeee.*

"What's the matter—train coming?"

"Aaaiiiyyyeee!" he repeated.

"Hydrocephalics?"

"Suppose the current goes upstream and zaps you in the dick?"

I carefully unstraddled the rail, zipping up my pants.

We were staggering now, which made it hard walking on ties, but made it to Fargo, the next station, with time to spare. When the train came we rode it three more stops, then walked east to the beach. By then a metallic sheen had spread from the auras of streetlights to the sky. In the faint blue light over the lake we were amazed at how filthy the beach was before the early crews arrived to clean it. Wire baskets overflowed. Piles of smashed cartons, cans, and bags littered the sand. It looked like the aftermath of a battle.

We began mounding garbage at the lapping edge of water the way kids mound sand for castles. A disk of new sun was rising across the lake from the general direction of Indiana. Two nuns, dressed in white with wimples like wings sprouting from their heads, glided past us and smiled.

"*And the dawn comes up like thunder,*" Harry was singing.

We took our clothes off and lit the pyre of paper and cartons. Its flames flicked pale and fragile-looking against the sun and foil of water. We sprinkled on the last swallow of whiskey and danced around the fire, then took turns starting back in the sand and running through the blazing paper into the lake.

The squad car came jouncing over the sand just as I was digging in for another sprint. One of the cops was out before the car even stopped. He missed a tackle as I raced by him into the flames, splashing out into the water. I stayed under as long as I could, then just kept stroking out. They followed me in the car along the breakwater, loudspeaker announcing that if I would come back we could talk it over.

When I woke it was noon. I was on my bathroom floor with the mat tucked over me. In the next room Harry was saying to the landlord, "Death . . . It stinks of death in here . . . corruption . . . putrescence . . . rotting flesh . . . abandoned bones. . . . What kind of charnel house are you running here anyway?"

The janitor arrived and removed a mouse from behind the refrigerator. And sometime later a coroner told me one of the most awful deaths he'd seen was that of a man who'd urinated on the third rail.

As far as I could see, the restaurant didn't have a name except maybe Drink Coca-Cola. I went in because it had an awning—forest green with faded silver stripes. It was cranked down, shading the plate-glass window from the corona of setting sun. Forty-seventh had a number of places like it, mostly family-owned, bars that served hot lunches, little restaurants different ethnics ran, almost invisible amid McDonald's arches and Burger King driveways.

I sat on the padded stool, revolving slightly, watching the traffic go by on Western, knowing if I could eat I'd get my rhythm back and things would be all right. I picked the mimeographed menu from between the napkin dispenser and catsup bottle. Nothing unusual: hamburgers, hot beef sandwich and mashed potatoes, pork chops. Handwritten under SOUPS was *Homemade Sauerkraut Soup.*

I'd never had sauerkraut soup before. I'd been thinking of *zupa,* but of something more medicinal, like chicken rice. "Homemade" sounded good. How could sauerkraut soup be otherwise, I thought. Who would can it?

"Yeah, ready?" the waitress asked. She was too buxom to be grandmotherly.

"Sauerkraut soup."

She brought it fast, brimming to the lip of the heavy bowl, slopping a little onto the plate beneath it. It was thick and reddish, not the blond color of sauerkraut I'd expected. The kind of soup one cuts into with the edge of the spoon. Steaming. The spoon fogging as if with breath. The peppery smell of soup rising like vapor to open the bronchial tubes. I could smell the scalded pepper and also another spice and then realized what colored the soup—paprika.

After a few sipped spoonfuls I sprinkled in more salt and oyster crackers for added nourishment. The waitress brought them in a separate bowl.

Sometimes I wonder if that place is still there on the corner of Forty-seventh. I like to think it is—hidden away like a hole card. I daydream I could go back. Drive all night, then take the bus to the factory. Open my old locker and my coveralls with STEVE stitched over the pocket would be hanging on the handle of the push broom. Walk in the grass down Western Boulevard. Sit at the counter sipping soup.

Outside, the crepe-paper colors were fading into a normal darkness. A man with a hussar's mustache, wearing a cook's apron, was cranking up the awning with a long metal rod. Neon lights were blinking on. I ordered a second bowl. I was never happier than in the next two years after I'd eaten those bowls of soup. Perhaps I was receiving a year of happiness per bowl. There are certain mystical connections to these things. Only forty cents a bowl. With my paycheck in my pocket, I could have ordered more, maybe enough for years, for a lifetime perhaps, but I thought I'd better stop while I was feeling good.

Charity

The agency assigned me to a slum on the South Side. There, among catastrophes, I encountered a small problem everyone faces in one way or another. People kept hitting me for handouts. Walking around the shabby streets in my white skin and blue suit made me appear wealthy. I *was* relatively rich.

Sometimes a group of black guys my own age standing outside the Record Shack gesturing and laughing would see me coming and spread out across the sidewalk. By the time I got there they were staring in stony silence—some jiving blankly to the music, some amused, a few openly hostile.

"Hey, social worker, you got some loose change?"

"I wanna buy me some cigarettes, man."

"Gimme a quarter."

After a while I realized they didn't want the money so

much as they wanted to see how I'd react: scared that if I didn't give they'd kick my ass, or would I try to be cool and joke it off ("Money, man? I'm paid in food stamps!"), or would I be professional and, digging out my wallet, distribute cards instructing them where to go for adult-education classes (maybe then they *would* kick my ass, waiting on the creaky fourth-floor landing of some mine-shaft dark tenement)? Or maybe I wouldn't say anything, just walk on by, as the caseworker ladies did sometimes—downcast eyes, smiling the martyr's half smile—and they'd watch her hips swing into the distance, discussing whether or not she was out here looking for it.

Sometimes some drunk would latch on to me, follow me down the street clutching at my elbow, stumbling, slobbering, explaining he was colored and I was white and what the hell did I know about it, and he was old and I was young and, man, when you're old everything hurts every minute. Telling me anything he could think of, all the memories and stories flooding into his head through the sluice of alcohol, but always amounting to the same tragedies and hard luck, the same line manufactured out of past realities: he needed winter clothes for his little baby, or money for carfare so he could get a job or for his TB—here he'd cough up a hoker and lay it on the sidewalk, green among pecking crowds of pigeons.

A few had a better approach: Look, man, I ain't gonna bullshit ya, I need it for a drink. Maybe they'd walk away if you shook your head no. But many were persistent, believing if they just bugged you long enough you'd pay to get rid of them. And if that didn't work they'd beg because if there's one thing a man can't stand it's another man begging him—particularly in public with everybody watching.

For lunch I'd usually go to McDonald's. It was a drive-in, all glass, tile, and stainless steel gleaming under neon. I didn't have a car but there were benches where you could sit outside and eat your hamburger and fries. Across the street the city was moving mountains of tenements. PARDON THIS INCONVENIENCE. ANOTHER IMPROVEMENT BEING MADE FOR A GREAT CHICAGO. RICHARD J. DALEY, MAYOR, the signs said. Workmen drove muddy, yellow bulldozers over fields of rubble. Drills clacked their prophecies of new foundations while kids chased up and down the huge mounds of dirt around the excavation pits. Blocks behind the site, modern high-rise housing projects rose up like walls. Usually a bunch of kids would come up and mooch dimes off me for Cokes. After they bought them they'd stand around discussing the White Sox with me, munching the ice when the drink was gone.

When I was new to the job—my first few months—constantly getting hit for money used to bother me. First I tried the open-handed approach and gave something to whoever asked. Usually all they wanted was a quarter. But I guess the word got out because everybody on the street began asking me for money. Each day I was out there, the same people would show up. The handouts began adding up. But what was worse, I worried about being thought of as something no self-respecting caseworker wants to be thought of as—a sucker.

So then I made myself judge. Decided I'd give money only to people who really looked as if they needed it. To whoever needed it! This, of course, was symptomatic of getting so close to the madness of the slum that your actions become absurd. But my absurdity was accepted by the neighborhood as something to be expected. When I'd refuse to shell out they argued: "Look, man, I know you gave something to Clyde Jones. How come you give to him and not me? Is he a better friend, man? His problems bigger than mine? Or how 'bout yesterday! Lucy Winters says you laid half a buck on her. What she doin' that I ain't?"

I could have said, "Look, man, it's my money to do

what I want with." But somehow this seemed to lead down the the-Lord-giveth-the-Lord-taketh-away path of Miss Newguard's lectures.

Miss Newguard had a repertoire of lectures painstakingly collected over many years of service. Each new worker got to hear the one about "And I'm sick and tired of hearing young people knocking the System in front of recipients when it's the System that puts clothes on their back and *yours* too!"

I'd dismissed her as just another of the frustrated old bitches the System was full of, who'd been rewarded for years of mediocrity and compliance with supervisory positions. It wasn't until the day I heard her lecture in Intake that I realized the extent of her power. The lecture began with a command for silence—her throat cleared into a pinched Kleenex—while all around her unwed mothers shushed illegitimate children.

"I hope none of you down here can work because if you can you won't get a cent out of *us*. I have to work for my money; you don't think the taxpayers pay me for staying home and having babies, do you? Of course not. If you are found eligible for public aid you will be expected to cooperate with our many programs to rehabilitate you. After all, friends, public aid, though a privilege of our great country, is not charity. We don't want you to feel like you're receiving a dole—no one with any pride wants that—feel rather that we are making an investment in your future and through that in the future of democracy."

I needed another approach but there never seemed time enough to figure one out. It was a minor problem—one that didn't pertain to the majority of my cases. Most of the requests came from their friends and neighbors—cripples, old people, kids, addicts, con men—all those who had failed to qualify or who had successfully avoided the welfare rolls. When my clients asked me for money it was usually as a loan, which they insisted on paying back. They weren't interested in testing me. They needed the money, maybe for a pair of shoes for the kid who was starting Head Start or just for a pack of cigarettes at the end of the month when the money from their unbelievably small aid checks ran out.

There never seemed to be time to figure out an approach to anything. The office was a madhouse. My desk tottered beneath stacks of ragged case records I was always going to read.

> Name: Florence Harper
> Case #: ADC 1795502
> Address: 3915 Cottage Grove
> Birthplace: Greenwood, Mississippi

After clearing a space to write on I'd sit and try to concentrate on a letter to the mental-health service worded strongly enough so that Florence Harper might be moved up a few ranks in the infinite line of people waiting for free therapy. I had to be careful not to word it too strongly so that when it passed under the bifocaled inspection of the archenemy, my supervisor, she didn't initiate proceedings to remove the children from the home. Such proceedings would never conclude. Their only effect was to divert energy away from dealing with the problem; their only purpose was to cover the supervisor in case something should happen. The telephones rang constantly like burglar alarms, as if we were in a continual process of being robbed. Occasionally the hysterical voice of a caseworker could be heard above the din, shouting into the phone that he had been ordered to hold the client's check because she had not shown up for housekeeping training.

> Dear Mental-Health Service:
>
> I am writing in reply to your letter regarding ADC 1795502. A waiting period of six months before therapy is inconceivable given

> the current situation. Mrs. Harper undergoes weekly "epileptic fits," which have been diagnosed as possibly hysterical in nature. In recent interviews she has become increasingly despondent and has indicated powerful anxiety associated with past experiences. She was fucked frequently by her father between the ages of twelve and sixteen. Her two oldest children are reportedly his. Her husband, a man thirty years older than Mrs. Harper, is threatening desertion because he can no longer support her and the children plus his family of ten by a previous marriage. Unknown to Mrs. Harper, her oldest son, Charles, a boy of twelve who is still in fourth grade, offered to blow the caseworker for a quarter during the last home visit. Due to rapid deterioration of the home

It was always at such a point that my phone would ring. Perhaps it would be Mrs. Harper herself calling as she did at least once a week to tell me she was going to kill herself and the kids.

"Don't, Mrs. Harper."

"Why not? What we got to live for?"

"Things will get better."

"You crazy! I'm gonna turn the gas on and kill us all!"

"Please don't do it, Mrs. Harper."

"I'm gonna do it this time for sure."

"But your children want to live."

"How do you know?"

"Anybody can see that . . . they're great kids. You've done your best raising them so far. They love you."

"They ain't happy—they just ain't sure how bad it is yet. I can't get 'em nothin'. They lucky if they got enough to eat."

"But you give them love."

"Love! What good's that without something to eat, some new clothes once in a while like other kids get?"

"You can't just give up."

"I sure can. My head hurts all the time, all I do is cry and worry about my kids—that they'll grow up like me. My head keeps hurtin'. You my worker. You suppose to do somethin'."

I tried to do something. I talked a friend of mine, a psychiatrist with a private practice, into giving her a half hour of his time a week free. I paid the fifty-cents carfare and two-fifty child care that it cost for her to get there. This arrangement lasted about a month and then she stopped going to see him.

"What the hell happened, Bill? You were supposed to do something," I complained.

"I tried to," he said, "but going back to that environment screwed everything up. Analysis is for the middle class, man. What she needs to solve her problems is fifty bucks more a week."

"Why'd you stop going?" I asked Florence Harper.

"It was wastin' the money," she said. "Nothin' but talk. Besides, that man is crazy. He tole me not to feel so bad about what my daddy done to me."

Walking downstairs from her apartment, I almost trip over Charles Harper sitting crouched on a stair beside the banister. He's holding himself as if he's got a stomachache.

"What are you doing here, Charlie?"

"Listening. Look what I got." He holds up a new-looking transistor radio. The earplug dangles from his ear.

"Nice . . . One of those Japanese ones?"

"You wanna know how I got it, right?"

"Uh."

We step out of the piss-damp hallway. The sun bounces into our eyes off windshields and windows.

"I didn't steal it—heh-heh—it's a present."

He stares up at me, the eyelids of his translucent twelve-year-old face wizened by sunlight. He winks. "You dig? What kinda music you like?" He turns the little radio on full blast and won't talk anymore, strolling past other kids down the street, dangling earplug plugged back in.

Once, after hours, I went to a bar to hear Muddy Waters with a friend of mine who'd started out with the agency but ended up working full time for the Movement. We'd both been drinking a lot all afternoon. It was hotter than hell at the end of August and we were drinking cold beers and at the point where after every beer you have to get up and piss. Muddy was great, singing one blues after another, sweat beaded on his face, his sport shirt hanging out. All the instruments were electric and they kept blowing fuses, so they had to turn the air conditioner off. The drummer worked before a microphone; the guy on harp cupped it against a microphone and when he fanned it the cord lashed around, so it looked as if he were playing an instrument with a long black tail. They had the doors open at both ends of the bar to catch the draft. It wasn't very dark yet. The windows still held some orange. The bar was loud and packed with a few couples trying to dance pressed against the wall and dripping beer bottles being passed over the heads at the bar. Kids squirmed through the tunnel the bar stools made on the pretense of wanting to shine shoes. After getting back from a trip to the john I find this guy in my seat talking in Al's ear. Al's just sitting there smiling, with his money spread out before him on the bar.

"Give me a buck, man. C'mon, brother, this is one of your own askin' ya. . . . Don't be a cheap mother. We got to help each other. I'm thirsty too, man. Fifty cents? . . . Okay, just buy me a beer."

Al says, "Don't bother me, man. I don't have time for that shit."

The guy shrugs and moves down the line.

I tried it in the district a few times and it worked pretty well on drunks. There was something cavalier about the "I don't have time for that shit" part that got them. But it obviously wasn't an all-around technique. The Reversal was even more limited—just as the guy has his timing down and is about to ask you for something you turn and face him eye to eye with your palm extended and say, "Hey, friend, can you spare two bits?"

What I finally did arrive at was a commonsense approach. Somebody would hit me for money and I'd say, "Look, man, I'd like to help you but do you have any idea how many times a day I get asked out here? If I started giving to everybody who asked me I'd have to be a millionaire."

That usually worked. It was much better than asking, "Why should I?" because then they'd say, "'Cause you got something extra and I ain't got enough." It had the effect of depersonalizing the request, of lumping them in with a group, which made it seem like the odds were against me.

But the best thing about it was that I believed it the most. There was the part about "I'd like to help you." That was true. I would. And yet it was realistic. I was making about five hundred dollars a month before taxes and the caseworkers were getting ready to go on strike. Who knew how long a strike might last? I had nothing saved. My rent was one hundred and ten dollars a month. I ate my meals out. I was paying one hundred a month for tuition, going to grad school full time at night in order to stay out of the draft. Whatever was left disappeared, mostly on drinking. If I got hit for a quarter five times per day and was in the field three times a week and about forty-nine weeks a year . . . I was entertaining the thought of the agency's giving us so much per month to give to moochers just the way they reimbursed us for transportation expenses. I mentioned the idea to Joe Faigabank, who was union treasurer.

"We can't ask them to do that," he said.

"Why not? Don't you have to loan out money when you're out in order to do your job sometimes?"

"Yeah, but look, trace the idea out to its logical conclusion. If you can do that why can't you just go out there and start giving the money away? You give the caseworker a wad and he just walks around poor neighborhoods handing it out. Even the Commies wouldn't support that."

"At least I'd know what the hell I'm supposed to be doing out there."

"You're supposed to be rehabilitating the disadvantaged by filling out forms in triplicate," Joe said.

"And looking for their boyfriend's shoes under the bed. Well, bring it up at the next meeting anyway, will you?"

Joe just stood there for a while punching staples in a case record. When he figured enough time had elapsed to convince me he'd thought it over he said, "Okay, figure it out and write up some statistics."

"When do you think we're going out on strike?"

"They're going to discuss it at the next meeting," Joe said. "They gotta give us more bread, man. I'm barely making it."

"Can you believe it's possible for an ADC mother with five kids to make it on two hundred and fifty, man?"

"Has to be something on the side. Boyfriends. That's the only way. The people who make up those budgets have PhDs in home economics."

"We ought to get the recipients out on strike with us."

"What, a hunger strike?"

Fuck it, I thought, if we don't strike I'm quitting. It had been a year and a half now that I'd been representing the bureaucracy, promising people aid they never got, jobs when there weren't any, medical care from butchers, sending them to psychologists who tried to help them accept their poverty, poking my nose in, spying—that's what the job basically was, spying. But hell, I thought, at least I'm trying to do something. Then Alma Richardson called me up.

Actually she had called me up about a month before and asked me to drop over. She wanted some advice. She was a lovely, gentle woman whose husband had deserted her five years ago, leaving her with four kids to support. She had worked in a factory stuffing jockstraps in boxes until she was knocked down by a lift truck and her spine was injured. Somehow the company screwed her out of getting any compensation. We were friends, or, as Miss Newguard preferred saying, we had rapport. My first winter as a caseworker, I had been very lucky in helping Mrs. Richardson out of a jam she should never have been in.

It had been a very bad winter with many spells of zero weather. Mrs. Richardson had made the mistake of moving from a condemned building. Her case record was lost and her aid checks went undelivered. When she first contacted me her new landlord had given her a five-day eviction notice. She'd been surviving for two months on what she had been able to borrow from relatives and friends, most of whom were little better off than she was. Her apartment had no furniture—some boxes and a mattress on the floor, a hot plate, but no refrigerator. She had been keeping her perishable foods on the windowsill, pulling them in at intervals so they wouldn't freeze, until someone got wise and stole them. I managed to talk the landlord into turning her heat back on and temporarily lifting the eviction notice. When I went to the office her case had supposedly been transferred from, I found her case record and checks among the myriad memos that had accumulated on the desk of her previous caseworker. He had quit over a month before and still hadn't been replaced. I had a violent argument with my supervisor, who took the position that since Mrs. Richardson had managed to exist for two months without aid then apparently she didn't need it. She was overruled, however, and the agency also approved fifteen dollars for a refrigerator. Her landlord, astounded at receiving his back rent, got us a good deal on a hot Frigidaire.

Mrs. Richardson trusted me. She wanted some advice on her ten-year-old son, Kevin. He had a hernia, she explained, and she wondered whether she should have corrective surgery performed now or wait until he was older. I told her that was strictly a medical decision, which I couldn't make, but that I did know that scar tissue heals faster at a young age. We talked about the possible effects growing up with a hernia might have on the boy, such as affecting his interest in sports or his entrance into puberty. I advised her to discuss it with a doctor. When I returned to the office I wrote out a referral to County Hospital for Kevin and mailed it to Mrs. Richardson.

This time I didn't recognize her voice at first.

"Who am I speaking to, please?"

"This is Mrs. Richardson." Her voice was flat and hollow at the same time.

"How are you, Mrs. Richardson? How did Kevin make out? Did he have his operation?"

"Yes."

"How's he doing?"

"He's dead."

I had an impulse to hang up. The phones were ringing. "He's dead? How could he be dead from a hernia operation? It's not that serious." For some reason I didn't believe her.

"He's dead," she said. "That's all I know. He died on the operating table."

"But how? Didn't they tell you how?"

"I guess they did. They said they had to cut a hole in his throat but that it didn't work. I don't know. I didn't understand them."

"I'm sorry," I said.

"I'm calling to find out about the funeral," she said. "Are you all gonna pay for it?"

"Yes . . . Tell the undertaker to call me and I'll make out the forms. . . . I'm sorry, Mrs. Richardson."

"Thanks," she said, and hung up.

I listened to the phone buzz for a while and then dialed County Hospital. I asked for information about Kevin. They gave me the runaround until I started hollering about an investigation. I didn't tell them I was a caseworker. I said I was with the mayor's office. A doctor explained that the boy had had a heart defect that had gone undetected and his heart had failed during the operation. They'd done all they could—performed a tracheotomy and massaged his heart—but he died. There was nothing anybody could do, he said. It was one of those things.

I hung up and my phone rang almost immediately.

"This is Mrs. Richardson again. I hate to bother you but on our budget for next month . . . Do you have to take Kevin off right away? I could use his twenty-five dollars to buy us some clothes for the funeral."

"I'll leave him on," I said.

"Thanks," she said. "I appreciate it."

I was coming back from the funeral. It was early in spring and tiny blades of grass were pushing up from mud, through broken glass from beer bottles, among cracks in the sidewalk. Papers that had been buried in snow dried yellow and blew around. It was my last day in the district. Joe Faigabank asked me to organize my ideas on a handout fund before I quit. He figured it would be a little something extra the union could concede over the bargaining table. Rumors of a public-employees' strike against the agency continued to circulate. Newspapers carried articles predicting riots in the black community during the coming "long, hot summer."

I thought on my last day I would remember my first day and see everything vividly again, but I didn't. I was walking down the street calculating one quarter times five per day times three days per week times forty-nine weeks per year times how many years per life when I saw this panhandler coming toward me a block away. I see him getting ready to mooch and automatically prepare my excuses: I'd like to help you, man, but do you realize how much I'd be spending if I gave to everyone who asked for it? Not just you, man, but all the charities for orphans and war victims and mental illness and cancer and the Heart Fund and kidney disease and the Panthers and the Peace Movement and I'm hardly making it myself, brother.

No socks. At half a block I see his red-rimmed eyes behind cracked, foggy glasses, a crushed hat, baggy pants with dragging, frayed cuffs, a too-thin, even for this spring day, topcoat, limping like a scarecrow assembled at a Goodwill store. He blinks at me and says, "Can you give me one cent?"

Horror Movie

He hadn't really been frightened until he went into the bathroom and saw the blood all over the toilet seat, streaks of it running down the bowl, filling in the cracks between the floorboards. He wanted to believe the old Puerto Rican lady from upstairs who'd told him not to worry, that it was just trouble some women have when they're pregnant. The old woman had been waiting for him when he got home late from school after exploring the new neighborhood. She told him the ambulance had just left with his mother. She said his mother had been worried about him, but the ambulance wouldn't let her stay. He was supposed to go inside and wait for Earl, but he could stay with her if he wanted. She kept lapsing into Spanish, and Calvin went inside to wait, trying not to worry.

But the blood was everywhere, dark clots of it, darker and stickier than blood should look, on the towels wadded in the sink, turning the water in the toilet bowl pink and clouded with what looked either like pieces of tissue or shreds of toilet paper. His first thought was that the old lady had lied, that his mother was dead, that Earl had killed her. Their constant arguing broke like a scab in his mind: how the whole reason they'd had to move was because the caseworker had caught Earl living with them and stopped their check. After that his mother had told Earl to work or get out and when she started flinging his stuff out the door he'd grabbed her by the throat, knocking Calvin aside like a fly when he tried to defend her. She had told Calvin, once they moved, no more Earl, but a few days later he was back living with them.

He went into his room and tried playing the basketball game he'd transplanted from their old apartment—shooting a rolled-up sock through a looped clothes hanger—hooking and dribbling, the crowd cheering, the sock flying around the walls, the Big C working the ball downcourt, taking a pass from James in the corner, driving, jumping, pumping. But he couldn't get the hanger to stick right in the molding. Every time he took a shot it fell, ending the game, leaving him thinking about his mother and the blood in the bathroom. Finally, he lay down on his bed and squashed the pillow down on his head, praying, "Jesus, help us," over and over till the feathers inside roared around his burning ears and he sprang up, suffocating. He thought he'd heard Earl come in and got up to check, but there was nobody there, so he walked out to the back porch.

Down in the alley the big guys were playing basketball. He watched them till the sun sank past the garage roofs, making the broken bottles gleam like copper, thinking of guys he'd known in school who'd been taken out of their homes and sent to orphanages and foster homes. The streetlights came on. Beyond the block of roofs and junkyards a moon the size of a basketball hung over the high-rise housing project. When the game broke up he went back inside.

He opened the refrigerator, its frosty light bulb throwing a pale slab of light. He left the door open till he'd lit the gas burners on the stove. The people who'd moved had taken the fluorescent tubes from the overhead fixture. The blue light flickering off the walls like a police flasher made noises seem too loud—the jelly jar striking the table, the tangled utensils rattling as he felt through the drawer for a table knife, careful of the butcher-knife blade, which always made him nervous. He ate his sandwich quickly, standing by the sink, washing it down with a Nestlé's Quik, letting the water jet from the tap, churning the top to froth like a chocolate malt. He locked the back door, not latching the chain so just in case Earl came he wouldn't think Calvin was trying to lock him out. Then he put out the lights and walked down the long hallway with the bathroom at one end and his room off the middle, into the living room to watch TV. In the dark it looked as if someone were sitting on the couch. He flicked on the lamp. A pair of Earl's trousers were flung over the cushions.

The late news was on, with a special report on Vietnam War victims. Every so often the picture would jump into blinking black-and-gray diagonals, and he'd have to get up to adjust the knobs and move the antennae around. He knew once the set got too warm he'd lose the picture for good, but he hoped it would play long enough for him to see part of his favorite show, *Monsters Till Midnight*. It came on every Friday, old horror movies, most of which were pretty funny, but Earl wouldn't let him watch it anymore ever since his nightmares started and he'd wet the bed. Once, after that, when Earl came in drunk and his mother wasn't home, Earl had started messing around, coming at him with his arms stretched out stiff, rolling his eyes, and working his hands as if he were going to strangle him. Calvin had run into his room and Earl had stood on the other side of the door yelling, "See what that Frankenstein shit done to your head! What you doin' in there? Pissing in your pants?"

He knew he shouldn't watch it now, but that seemed better than just sitting up doing nothing but waiting. The commercials were running and he was feeling jittery, like sitting in a roller coaster before the ride really started but it was already too late to get off. He turned the sound down and sat near the set so he could flick it off if Earl suddenly came in.

Lightning flashed over an old castle and an organ played weird, shaky music. A team of wild-looking black horses clattered over wet cobblestones, dragging an empty black stagecoach behind them. Their enormous eyes rolled and they tossed at their bits, racing under dark trees, galloping through a graveyard, the coach careening off tombstones behind them. HaHaHaHaHaHa mad laughter streamed through the night. Calvin heard something at the door and jumped up, punching the OFF button.

He stood there, the silver dot in the middle of the screen seeming to take forever to fade, waiting for Earl to come in, but he didn't. Calvin went to the door and stood there listening. It was quiet, but every time he decided he'd been mistaken he heard a creak like someone shifting his weight on the other side of the door as if he were listening to Calvin too. He sank slowly to his haunches and tried to peer through the keyhole, but it was stuffed with fuzz. He put his ear to it, listening hard for breathing, but he couldn't be sure he heard any. Finally he crawled away from the door, trying not to make a sound. He was sweating and knew he didn't want to watch the show anymore, but he turned the set back on. It flashed into a rolling series of lines; he turned up the sound. Then he forced himself to walk loudly, whistling past the front door, stop, and ask in his toughest voice, "Who's there?"

No one answered.

"Ain't nobody at the door, Daddy," he yelled back into the living room.

He turned the set off, removed his shoes, and sneaked past the front door into his bedroom. He undressed in the dark and covered himself up although he was warm. Beneath the covers he brought his knees up and reached under his pillow for his wooden cross. He'd kept it there ever since the night last spring that he and his best friend, James, had gone to the Adelphi and seen a vampire movie. What had frightened him most were the rats swarming across the screen through the sewers, their countless eyes a piercing red, squealing and scrambling over one another's bodies like a current of slimy fur and leathery tails, rushing from the pipes out into the streets, swarming through the windows, twitching snouts and yellow buckteeth filling the screen, almost bursting through the screen itself like circus animals through a paper hoop. They were the vampire's rats overrunning the village and only a cross had turned them back. He and James agreed it was the best movie they'd ever seen, but later that night he'd sensed the rats crawling about his room, waiting for their forces to gather before pouncing on his bed. And he knew they were real, having seen them often enough before, remembered the stench of death that had driven them out of their apartment the summer one died in the wall, and his mother screaming in the middle of the night when one came out of the bathroom and the next day putting out little bottle caps of poison all over the house and telling him he'd die if he touched them. And the time the baby of the lady downstairs had his lower lip chewed away, and later there had been a march through the streets with everyone angry and singing at the same time and the leaders had carried huge rats nailed to sticks above their heads like flags.

All that was in the old neighborhood before he'd had

the cross. Getting the cross had been James's idea. They'd copped it from a religious-goods store downtown. He lay there thinking about James and himself walking the streets after school, sneaking under the turnstiles and riding the El downtown to see a movie or if they didn't have the money just running through the crowded stores.

Then he was dreaming and in his dream he and James were racing up the down escalators, going higher and higher, past chandeliers, overlooking each floor, merchandise spread out as far as the eye could see. The people riding down were all giving them dirty looks. He knew they'd tell the store detective. Then they were so high there weren't any more things to buy, just offices with frosted doors and the sound of typewriters, and up even higher, with the escalator changing from smooth gliding steel to one with old rubber steps and black beltlike handrails that jerked along. James had managed to stay in front no matter how hard Calvin tried to catch up, and every so often James would turn back and grin.

He reached the top, where the escalator folded into a bare wooden floor. He stood in a huge dim room, dusty light gleaming through dirty windows, and barely visible through the windows were the smoky tips of skyscrapers. It was some kind of storeroom, full of crates and rolls of material.

"Hey, James, where are you, bro?" he called. But James didn't answer. He walked down an aisle of boxes, half blinded by the sun against the window at the end.

"Hey, James!" he called again. He heard something move down the next aisle and suddenly remembered the store detective and here he was giving himself away by shouting. At the same instant his heart started pounding so hard he was paralyzed, like a man having a heart attack. He heard a hiss and looked up. James was standing on top of a stack of boxes that towered among the cobwebbed rafters.

"Hey, Cal," he started to say, and then the detective rose up behind him, holding an ax with both hands over his head and bringing it down with a cracking noise through James's skull, pitching him headlong off the boxes, James tumbling down and striking the floor all bouncing arms and legs beating up dust.

Calvin ran over to him, crying, "James! James!" James lay twisted on his face. One of his legs had come off and there was a jagged hole in the back of his head showing the hollowness inside. And then Calvin realized he was looking at a mannequin—one of those chocolate-looking ones that are supposed to be Negro. Besides, it couldn't be James, it was wearing a dress. He twisted its head around and its wooden eyelids clunked open like a doll's, the doll looking up at him with his mother's eyes from his mother's face. He heard a laughing scream and saw the detective, framed against the blurry blazing window, running up the aisle toward him, ax poised above his head, and felt his heart pound loose in his chest as he tried to rise.

He woke drenched with sweat, someone shaking his bed, until he realized it was his heart pounding so hard it felt as if it were shaking the room. He lay forcing his face into the mattress, clenching his teeth until his jaw ached, trying to regain control. He needed to breathe, to suck in lungfuls of air, but was afraid of moving in the dark. He knew he had to pretend to sleep. If someone was in the room with him, standing over his bed, then his only chance was stillness. If he didn't move, didn't acknowledge the presence by showing his fear, he might be overlooked.

He pretended to sleep a long time, listening to the silence, analyzing the steady stream of creaks and rustlings. His body seemed glued to the mattress by his sweat and he began to itch all over.

His left arm had gone totally numb. He slid his right arm under the pillow, feeling for the cross. It was gone.

He started to panic, sure someone had taken it away, then he touched it, stuck between mattress and wall. Holding it to his throat, he tried inching off the sweaty area, the sheets unpasting from his back. He reached down and snapped the sweaty elastic band on his shorts, which had been eating into his waist. The air in the room suddenly felt cool and a chill swept over him. He became conscious of having to urinate. His crotch felt so wet that he wasn't sure whether he'd pissed in his bed already or not.

He remembered the times he'd waited like this before, praying for the light, not daring to step out of bed for fear of rats. He'd always made it through to the morning, but his mother had always been in the next room too. He thought of sneaking upstairs and begging the old Puerto Rican lady to take him in, but he knew these were fantasies less real than his fears, that as soon as he moved through the doorway the detective would be waiting at the end of the hall, stalking from the bloodstained bathroom. His muscles clenched till they cramped, the tip of his penis aching, the ache spreading inside his body until the pain began to rival the fear, a part of the fear itself. He heard the back door rattle, then creak as if someone were in the kitchen, the sound so clear he wondered if it wasn't Earl in late, feeling his way drunk. But the thought of Earl sneaking around the house didn't ease the fear. Maybe it had been Earl behind the door all the time. Maybe this was Earl's way of getting rid of him. He could feel his hate and anger trying to well up through the fear, smothered by it each time, cursing the motherfucker oh motherfucker dirty mother you mother mama oh mama.

When he woke again it was Saturday noon. He slipped on his clothes and stripped off the bed sheet, stuffing it under the bed. The new urine stain darkened the yellowed edges of previous stains on the mattress.

He was so hungry he had a stomachache and he paced

the flat, opening drawers and looking through cabinets. He picked through Earl's crushed trousers and found a couple of crumpled dollar bills. He put his sunglasses on and went out the back door, leaving it unlocked behind him, the fall sun glinting off the worn back porches.

Calvin ran down the alley and up Division, change jingling in his pockets, trying to get as far away as he could. His breath came so easily that it felt as if he'd never tire, moving at a pace slightly faster than the crowd's, the reflection of his body running wavery beside him in store windows. He couldn't slow down, afraid he'd lose the feeling of excitement he felt out on the streets. He tried to figure out how to use the feeling. If he knew what hospital his mother was at he could go there or call her on the phone. Then he thought of trying to get back to the South Side and find James. That's what the feeling now was most like—feeling free on Saturdays, he and James going somewhere, maybe the Adelphi, sitting up in the balcony zinging flattened popcorn boxes through the projection beam, their shadows flying across the screen and everybody in the theater shouting and laughing.

He jogged the streets for a long time, finally jaywalking through traffic to where a group of people crowded around a carryout stand. Some of them were Puerto Ricans, like the kids at his new school, talking rapidly in Spanish. He could hear the grease popping and his stomach turned over. He ordered a Polish sausage with everything on it and a chocolate malt. He ate half of it walking down the streets, walking till he found a doorway in a boarded-up store where he could relax. Pigeons landed and he tossed them pieces of bun till he had them eating out of his hand. Then it started to get chilly and little whirlpools of dust blew out at him from the corners of the doorway, so he left.

He kept checking the street signs and fronts of buses for names he recognized and watching for buildings that looked like hospitals. His earlier feeling of freedom had dissolved into an aimlessness that bordered on panic. Even though it was still daylight neon lights were blinking on in the fronts of stores. The sidewalks were already in shadow. He became more and more aware of losing his invisibility as the crowds thinned and he tried not to look at cops, but kept meeting their eyes. At an intersection he noticed a movie marquee flickering little yellow bulbs and wandered over to check out the advertisements.

Half the bulbs were burned out and so many letters were missing on the marquee that he couldn't tell what was playing. There were no pictures in the glass cases; the cases themselves were dirt-fogged and pocked with BB holes. But taped to the door was a torn black poster announcing in dripping red letters

VOODOO VAMPIRE
If you frighten easily
DO NOT enter this theater!

He pushed one of his crumpled dollars through a slot in the glass booth and a faded violet ticket cranked out. An old junkie of an usher, one eye clouded pearl blue with a cataract, nodded at him as he tore the ticket in two. Calvin walked quickly across the empty tile lobby, through peeling arches and cracked pillars plastered with old posters of movies he'd never heard of, to a dim corner where an old woman sat behind a huge pile of popcorn heaped under a bare light bulb. He bought a box of popcorn and a box of Red Hots, then headed up the balcony stairs. The silence of the theater made him uneasy—outside he'd imagined sitting among screaming gangs of kids like at the Adelphi. Finally he reached the top and entered through a dirty velvet curtain.

He stopped immediately and waited for his eyes to readjust. There was a bluish beam slanting directly overhead from the projectionist's slot and the sound of running film, but nothing onscreen. He couldn't even see the screen, as if a dense wall of blackness were being projected. Then he heard the far-off booming of surf and gulls trading calls.

Two disks flaring gold were emerging onscreen. Calvin made his way down the steps in the reflected glow, feeling along the backs of seats till his hand touched a face.

"Sorry," he mumbled, veering to the other side of the aisle and stumbling into a lumpy stuffed seat amid an explosion of bird caws. At the same moment he became aware that the lights onscreen were actually the eyes of a black man watching the dawn.

Dawn broke all around the man now, his silhouette against pale golds and pinks, rocking in the bow of a longboat. He was chained like the others, all rowing in unison, while the whites sat in the stern, their muskets held ready. Raz, one of the other Africans called him, and he looked away from the horizon, where a square-rigger rode, toward where the man pointed to a green island jutting up from the sunrise-stained water.

The popcorn tasted a hundred years old, so stale it squeaked when he chewed it. Calvin sat there sucking the husks from his teeth, watching the movie: Raz and the rest of them marched through the jungle, were put to work in the cane fields. Calvin felt relieved and disappointed at the same time—the movie wasn't really frightening. About the only halfway-scary thing was the castle, which rose above everything, its dark stone draped in Spanish moss; women peered out from its shadowy balconies, elegant black women in hooped, billowing gowns, faces hidden by fans, holding their plumed floppy hats against the wind.

He let the popcorn box slide to the floor, then kicked it over, grinding the kernels under his feet. The floor seemed to attach itself to the soles of his gym shoes, slippery and sticky at the same time, as if the years had accumulated in layers of masticated caramel and decomposed Holloway bars. He sat unconsciously feeling stuck as he watched one of the slaves mired in quicksand. The man had been trying to escape through the swamps at night. He'd managed to grab on to a vine and had almost pulled himself free when the arms began shooting up through the slime all around him. Then came their heads—eyes without eyeballs, gray rotted flesh, tattered rags dripping and steaming in a ring of fox fire. The slave was screaming. Calvin could feel himself wanting to shout back like he would have, like everybody would have by now, at the Adelphi, but the theater remained silent. There were only the screams and gurgling as the man was sucked under, the film clicking through the sprockets, and a low throbbing like an enormous heartbeat, which Calvin suddenly realized had been going on for some time, growing steadily louder, coming from the castle.

He opened the box of Red Hots. His legs felt cold and he drew them up under him on the seat. The throbbing speeded up, grew louder. Calvin could feel it in his teeth. Filled with tension, he bunched himself up, peering into the midnight of the screen, trying to brace himself for whatever was coming.

The women ran shrieking down the grassy slopes between the castle and slave shacks, their nightgowns streaming, eyes mad, lips curled back into fang-baring smiles.

Calvin could almost feel their breath. They were horrible and yet he was unable to look away. He kept telling himself it would be over soon and he would watch just a little more despite the part of him that knew already that watching this movie was a terrible mistake and that urged him to tear himself from his seat and leave the theater now. He juxtaposed an inner image of himself against the huge images on the screen: he lay stiffened with fear in his bed while the women made their way down the hallway to his room.

Then it was over: Raz picking his way from shack to shack over the bodies of the men he'd landed with. They lay faceup, smeared with blood, eye sockets empty, skin gray as if it had been drained of color as well as of blood.

Calvin filled his mouth with Red Hots, wondering if the peppery candies could warm him up. The theater kept getting colder, as if someone had turned the air conditioner on full blast. A wind seemed to be swirling under the seats.

"Ohhh God, ooohh God," a voice was saying, then it gurgled off into a spasm of retching. At first Calvin tried to fit it in the film—the choking in between Raz's panting—but it seemed to come from directly behind him. Heaves like someone's insides were coming apart, so violent he was afraid to turn around. The Red Hots were gone and he started chewing the cardboard flaps of the box.

Raz had entered the castle. Scarlet draperies were flailing in a scarlet room. He moved past chandeliers and tapestries of wolves leaping at the throats of stags, through rooms lined with armor and weapons, across marble floors inlaid with strange symbols. A piano was playing a disjointed melody and he followed the sound till he came to the room where it stood, silent, no one at the keys.

An iron door swung slowly open. The women stood on the other side smiling. They filed out toward him, hands reaching out like claws in hideous supplication. He backed away, then suddenly whirled, seizing a sword from the wall and slashing it wildly before him, breaking through their circle, till he was through the door, pulling it shut against them.

He ran down a stone tunnel lined with fuming torches, up broken stone stairs, scattering rats, splashing through black puddles. The stairs spiraled higher and higher, curling back outside along the seaward wall of the castle, the waves smashing in far below, the wind howling through eaves. A skull-like moon sailed through smoking clouds. The stairs tapered into mere footholds, until at last he scaled the side of the highest turret, boosting himself in through a narrow window.

The moonlight streamed like a projectionist's beam through the window behind him. Sword poised, he stood silvered in the center of a low, tilted chamber peering into the shadows. It looked empty, only the wind whistling in over ledges of stone. Then, mixed with the wind, came another sound, like the hissing of a snake. In the farthest corner the vampire was unfolding from his black cape. He hung from the ceiling like an enormous insect, his skin so white it was luminous, pulsing from within with the whiteness of maggots. His eyes were ringed by hollows of red and a gaping hole of a mouth curled back, revealing long yellow fangs and a scaly gray tongue that flicked as he hissed. He began to circle the walls, eyes liquid red like an albino rat's, grinning at Raz's paralysis. When he reached the window he crouched as if about to take flight, his body blotting out the moonlight. Then, with a shriek, he whirled and sprang at Raz, the sword arcing to meet him, both connected for a moment, and then his hands unclasped from Raz's throat, his torso collapsing into a deflated heap of silks and ashes while his head toppled backward, rolling across the tilted floor.

It seemed to Calvin to roll out of the screen, to hang in midair even with the balcony, eyes still living, teeth gnashing and foaming up blood, flames starting to lick out of nostrils and eye sockets, screaming over and over in a voice that shook the theater, "*Kill Me! Kill Me!*"

Calvin held to the sides of his seat as he felt it begin to whirl. For a moment the seat seemed to pitch backward like a dentist's chair. His body had flinched as the head appeared to roll into space. He struggled like a dreamer half awakened from a nightmare of falling to regain his equilibrium and breath. The earsplitting screaming made him weak and nauseated; he couldn't understand how it could continue like a broken record. Where was the audience? Had the projectionist gone mad?

Calvin ducked his head between his knees and clapped his hands over his ears. He entered the world of the smell of the theater floor, the spearmint wrappers, the rancid popcorn oil, old urine, stale sweet wine. Above him it went on as if it would never end.

He felt a bony hand lock on the back of his neck.

"Hey, boy," the old usher said, his gums showing as he chuckled, "it's just a movie."

Calvin opened his eyes. The houselights were on, naked light bulbs dim among cobwebs, shining down from the filthy ornate dome of the empty theater. He looked around at the curving rows of dilapidated seats, their backs wadded with hardened gum. The screen hung down below, dirty white, looking small and flabby like a piss-stained sheet. He pushed himself up and limped up the aisle. His foot had fallen asleep. The usher was still grinning and grinding his toothless jaws, rolling over popcorn with a carpet sweeper. In the last row a ragged figure slouched forward over the back of a seat, a strand of bilious vomit dripping from his mouth.

"A winehead," the usher's voice said from a few rows below, tiny and unamplified in the empty expanse. "They come in here all the time to die."

Calvin turned to stare at him.

"Say, my man," the usher said, his cataract twinkling, "you ever had a gum job?"

"Huh?" Calvin said.

"A gum job, heh-heh!" He demonstrated, retracting his lips till his purple gums showed in a grin, munching softly together. "Dig? You old enough to get it hard?" He set his sweeper aside and trudged up the aisle toward Calvin.

Calvin forced himself to walk until he reached the

curtain, but as soon as he slipped through he was bounding down the stairs. He hurried through the lobby, instinctively braced for the bright sunlight after the darkness of the theater. Night came as a shock, bringing the images he'd just seen back in a rush. All he could think of doing was getting away from the theater.

He jogged down the sidewalks, past grated shop windows and padlocked doors, keeping to the best-lit streets, conserving his strength for sprints across dark alleys and doorways. The streetlights bounced above him as he ran, turning from time to time to check behind him, but the streets were empty except for a single figure blocks away.

He kept going till he came to a long viaduct. A train was *ding*ing, hissing out steam on the tracks above. Most of the bulbs in the tunnel were out and he stared through the darkness of crisscrossing girders, unable to see the other side.

The walls inside were cracked, the sidewalks strewn with hunks of concrete and broken bottles. He felt the presence of sewer rats sneaking along the gutters, of eyeless men moving toward him in stiff-legged strides. The train coupled overhead with a screech of metal wheels. Calvin spun and raced back out to the street. But the figure he'd seen blocks away was closer now, approaching, hunched under the streetlights.

He dashed down a dark side street where the streetlights seemed spaced farther apart, glowing down through a tangle of swaying branches. He ran a block and turned—nothing. But now he couldn't stop running. He had given the sign—his panic was an open admission of their existence. The movie informed the street like an afterimage. He could feel the women clutch after him from doorways as he rushed by.

He hurdled across an alley. A car with only its orange parking lights burning glided out after him, its spotlight sweeping the walls and trees along his path.

"Stop right there!" a cop hollered out the squad-car window. Calvin cut down a gangway between two buildings, across a backyard, the dog in the next yard enraged, barking at him along the fence. He flipped a low gate and took off down the alley, zigzagging as he ran, tensed for the gunshot, wondering if he could throw himself down before the slug tore into his back, an image of a kid his age sprawled in a puddle of blood on a magazine cover and the caption KILLED BY PIGS at the center of his mind. He made it to the intersection of the alley and a dark street lined with junkyards. He trotted low behind parked cars, avoiding the next street, which was well lit, knowing now he had to keep to the side streets with the cops looking for him. He was thinking again of the places they sent you—Audy Home, Good Counsel Orphanage, St. Charles Reform School.

He crossed over between parked cars at the next street, unable to run anymore, his side bursting and heart swollen so huge he was barely able to suck his breath past it. A bar's neon sign burned in the middle of the block. Music floated out down the street. Staring between parked cars, through the open door he could see people lined up drinking and shouting and a woman dancing on the bar in her underwear. A drunk groaned, passed out in a doorway. At the mouth of the next alley a man was bracing himself against a wall pissing and laughing at two other men. They had an enormous fat Puerto Rican woman tied to a phone pole with a shirt. Her face was smeared red with rouge and lipstick and she had a bloody nose. Their eyes met.

"Help," she said in English. She didn't yell, she hardly said it, just kind of formed the word with her lips, looking straight at him with terrified made-up eyes. One of the men kicked her when she said it. It wasn't a violent kick—he brought his foot up like a punter into her breast, which flopped up and hit her in the chin.

"Ooowww," she said, as if he had hurt her feelings.

"What you looking at, man?" the guy pissing said to Calvin.

Calvin kept on going. He knew none of them were afraid he'd try to help her, that even she didn't really expect it, that they all knew you couldn't help anyone unless you were big enough to hurt someone. He couldn't run anymore. He was shivering. The windshields of cars were fogged with vapor, their hoods wet as if it had rained. The streetlights had halos; mist hung over a block of rubbled lots and half-wrecked houses.

He looked back and caught a glimpse of a figure several blocks away jumping into a doorway. Maybe the guy who was pissing had decided to follow him just in case, he thought. He started walking fast, listening for footsteps behind him. He turned around again. This time he was sure he'd seen the same figure leap out of sight behind a tree. He was feeling sick. His mouth tasted sour and he spit, fighting to keep from vomiting. He turned the next corner, stopped, and peeked around the building. He was coming! The same hunched figure he'd seen earlier that night, running toward him now, in and out of the shadows of trees. It was hard for him to start running again. His legs had gone stiff. Help me, help me, his mind kept repeating with each breath.

He turned corners, dodged through parked cars, racing down the middle of empty streets, praying to see headlights, even the cops. At the end of a street a wall of high-rise housing projects reared up, lit in yellow. When he saw it he knew where he was and caught his second wind.

The street dead-ended and he ran through canyons of buildings, his gym shoes slapping in an echo chamber of walls. Yellow bulbs smoldered above green doors; everything looking locked, as if the world were hiding for the night. He could hear the wind knocking the wires against the flagpole. He leaped over a row of hedges, turning his head in midair as if suspended and glimpsing the figure still running behind him across the expanse of concrete, overcoat billowing, hair shining silver, then he hit the other side, staggering to regain his balance, back in stride, past swings and monkey bars, highfliers, teeter-totters, the playground floodlights projecting his giant fleeting shadow across a screen of concrete walls.

They were nearing the high cyclone fence that separated the playground from the street. All his efforts had been directed toward it since he'd seen the project. He knew where the mesh had been bent up at the bottom, just wide enough for him to roll under, but he didn't recognize the spot in the dark till he was right on it. He hit the ground, arms dragging the rest of his body clear, shirt hooked a fraction of a second till his momentum tore it loose, scrambling back up to run, his scraped knees on fire, then numb. Behind him he heard a body hit the fence so hard that the sound rang up and down the block. He glanced back and saw the figure spread-eagled against the mesh, clawing his way to the three strands of barbed wire at the top.

Calvin fled across the street, down the alley. He remembered having left the back door open, but realized it might be locked if someone had come home. He raced up the back stairs and pushed against the door; the doorknob turned and he was alone in the dark kitchen.

His hands were trembling so bad he could hardly lock the door. He slid down it and lay deafened by his own breathing and blood pounding through his head, trying to hear past it for footsteps climbing the back stairs. He fought to regain control, afraid his heaving would carry out into the alley. Slowly he became aware of his body again: instead of a single throbbing pain it divided itself into many, his head, his chest and side, his shaking legs, knees. He touched his knees through the tears in his jeans. Part of the material seemed ground into the skin; his kneecaps felt sticky and his own touch like a sting. He still hadn't heard any footsteps.

He sat on the floor in the kitchen wondering what to do next, thinking of sneaking down the hallway to his bedroom, climbing into bed deep under the covers with the cross against his throat. But the thought continued beyond his stopping it like a runaway reel of film, images of himself cringing in the dark, waiting night after night for the terrors pacing the flat.

His legs kicked out on their own, knocking over a chair. At the instant it hit he thought he heard someone exclaim in the front of the apartment. He held very still—there had been a click like the opening of a door. He became aware of a draft along the floor as if the front door were open. And then he realized that while he lay here gasping and listening at the back stairs they could have fooled him, could have come stalking up the front way through the silent hallways, listening at doors for him, peering through the cracks.

He got to his feet and made his way along the stove to the drawer where the silverware was kept. He opened the drawer and felt along the utensils, his fingers trailing over can openers, ladles, the potato masher, until they located the heavy blade.

He picked out the butcher knife and felt it balance in his hand, tested the razor-sharp thinness of the edge growing into the heavy thickness of the blade. His fingers fit perfectly along the wooden handle. It had taken him so long to pick it up and now he knew that he had always been right—to grasp it would be the final admission that everything was real. For a fraction of a moment he thought—suppose it was his mother, back from the hospital, moving down the hallway in her nightgown, or Earl, finally returned, but he knew it wasn't either. It was as if they had never existed.

He swung it gently in front of him, feeling the air swish

by, slightly resisting the blade and turning it in his hand, feeling the strength its heavy momentum imparted to his arm as he swung it again, cleaving the air before him, stepping into the long hallway, with each footstep cocking his arm and pumping, possessed by a new freedom as he hacked through darkness.

The Apprentice

As always, the boy could smell the blood of animals in the rain. Drops pummeled the old wooden station wagon while a single wiper blade saluted feebly against the flooded windshield. This was not how he'd imagined the city, dark as a blackout, thunder overhead like bombers. Wolfgang, cringing in back, wedged farther under the seat and began to whine.

"Can you believe a monster like that crying?" Uncle asked, and exploded into another coughing fit.

Uncle swung the wagon off the street, spitting out the window as rain blew in, gunning into an alley, up its clattering current of tin cans and rubbish. Waterfalls from rotted drainpipes sluiced through fire escapes as their headlights sped past.

When they stopped, the downpour flowed over them as if they were still speeding. Uncle killed the headlights, lit his snuffed-out cigar, and immediately began coughing again, smothering his face in his sleeve.

"This is it," he rasped, checking the rearview mirror as he repeatedly did to make sure they weren't being followed.

"This is what, Uncle?"

"*What, Uncle?* The restaurant!"

Reaching past him, Uncle rolled the window down and forced the boy's head out. Rain immediately flattened his hair, streamed down his face like tears, choking his nostrils. He stared into a cavernous doorway lit by a tiny orange bulb that glowed beneath a madly *ping*ing metal shade. Its light reflected off a sheet-metal door across which was spray-painted SPANISH BLADES. There were other names, hearts, slogans, obscenities, chalked and fading, but before he could make them out Uncle yanked him back in.

"What did it say, Zoltán?" Uncle often called him Zoltán when something important was happening.

"Spanish Blades."

"Like I told you. Now you know the secret. Where I make our deliveries. Where maybe someday you'll be a waiter. If anything happens to me, here's where you come."

"What could happen to you, Uncle?"

"Getting old, Zoltán. Getting old in a city of old Nazis. Every day they track you down a little more." He coughed and spit violently as if in final punctuation. "Goddamn!" he cursed as the spit dribbled on the window he'd once again forgotten to roll down.

The boy wanted to ask why the restaurant was here, in an alley among warehouses and factories; to say he wasn't sure he wanted to be a waiter. Up till tonight he hadn't been sure there even was a restaurant—though he'd kept that from Uncle. Now, at least, he'd seen the name, Spanish Blades, although it wasn't glowing in blue neon the way he'd pictured it from Uncle's description: *An exclusive restaurant, a private club, for all those who'd been excluded and had finally made their way here, to this city of displaced persons. Displaced persons, DPs, who'd come from the corners of the earth evading politics and poverty; draft dodgers, deportees, drifters, illegal aliens, missing persons, personae non grata, refugees, revolutionaries, and émigré royalty, all orphans, mingling beneath the same ensign in a dining room where chandeliers rotated a crystalline light and blue poofs of flame erupted as waiters, tuxedoed like magicians, ignited food.*

"And gypsy violins, Zoltán," Uncle would say, eyes magnified wildly behind the cracked spectacles he'd found on the highway, his accent propelling a spray of saliva. "Chefs! Gourmets! Einsteins of the belly—exiled like him—who would be lost without our deliveries! This is what we ride the highways for! But never tell anyone our secret mission!"

The city had not been what he'd expected, but after that night it was what he dreamed of. Oily streets dissolving ruby and emerald beneath traffic lights, a restaurant secret among warehouses, and finally the girl in the flicker of blue flames. Especially the girl.

He daydreamed of her for days afterward as they resumed "salvaging" the highways, Uncle behind the wheel, he and Wolfgang riding shotgun, scanning the flat road. It was a life he'd loved, the fields and woods emerging from mists, roosters breaking out of their cocoons of night, Uncle asking, "What is a rooster?" as if it were a riddle to be solved anew each sunrise.

A twig fire.

A fallen star in a barnyard.

And the road littered with the driftwood of night. Animals whose eyes had turned to quartz in the hypnosis of headlights, steamlike souls still hovering around their bodies. Rabbits, possums, coons, squirrels, pheasants—like a single species of highway animal. Some crushed beyond recognition, even their pelts useless and so left behind. But most still limp, waiting to be collected with the other highway scrap—blown tires like lizard skins, dropped mufflers, thrown hubcaps, lumber, hay bales, deposit bottles, anything that could fall off a tailgate or blow out of a car window.

There was always the hope of finding something special—once, a pistol that Uncle claimed was a murderer's because he could see fingerprints glowing on it in the dark. Another time the viola, still in its battered case, or, as Uncle insisted, its coffin. According to Uncle the viola in its coffin was an omen that they must bury their valuables. Everything was an omen to Uncle.

"Could you teach me to read omens?" the boy once asked.

"I have been all along," Uncle replied.

Uncle interpreted dreams, foretold weather, could read the future in the entrails of certain animals. Uncle knew everything about animals. He could rebuild them as he had Wolfgang's broken hind legs.

They'd found Wolfgang in a drainage ditch along the road. The boy yelled for Uncle to stop, thinking it was a dead fawn. When Uncle saw what kind of dog it was he was reluctant.

"Those are Nazi dogs. That dog is an omen of Nazi things to come."

But he'd given in to the boy's request. They carefully moved Wolfgang, splinted his legs, and Uncle made casts out of the papier-mâché he used for his models.

Uncle's skill came from rebuilding dead animals. His small taxidermy shop remained closed since his license had been revoked, but Uncle continued to work. A week before the trip to the city, the boy had watched him create his masterpiece, a strange bird assembled from the parts of many birds—hawk, heron, owl, plumes of cock pheasant and peacock, cardinal red, jay blue.

"I wish I could give it songs," Uncle said. "What would we make it sing like?"

"Meadowlarks," the boy said.

"Good. And whippoorwills, thrushes, doves."

The bird, wearing a newspaper hood, balanced on the front seat between them the night they drove into the city.

"Hold it tight," Uncle said as they roared down the alleys faster and faster, away from SPANISH BLADES. He hadn't turned on the headlights. They paused at the mouth of an alley to let a black-and-white sedan go by.

"*Polici,*" Uncle muttered.

The *polici* were something they worried about on the highways but seldom encountered. Uncle regarded the game wardens as a worse threat, especially a man named Kopf, who had been instrumental in closing his taxidermy shop. They took precautions. If they were stopped the boy was to be an idiot nephew, Malvolio the mute, and Uncle made him practice rolling his eyes and drooling. They also rehearsed throwing the Army blanket over whatever they'd collected in the back of the De Soto, and muzzling Wolfgang.

"*Polici* are not necessarily our enemies."

"Who are our enemies, Uncle?"

"*Who?* The same as those of all peoples. The *secret* police. The KGB of the soul, CIA of the brain, SS who think they are only harmless dogcatchers. Game wardens persecuting a man who do not know themselves they are a branch of the Gestapo. KKK, FBI, ICBM, DDT, initials! Initials are our enemies, Tadeusz."

Uncle pulled the wagon into an abandoned lot behind a tattered billboard. They adjusted the hood over the bird and, holding newspapers over their heads, ran across the puddled street, leaving Wolfgang behind to cower and guard.

They shouldered open a warped door and stumbled up a crooked stairway. A string ran along the banister and when Uncle tugged it a light bulb swung on at the head of the stairs.

Uncle huffed and coughed more with each stair. At the top he stood swaying against the door, balancing the bird, its talons clutching his wrist as if perched.

A buxom woman in a kimono, makeup congealed in the wrinkles around her eyes, opened the door a crack and stared out at them. Her hair was dyed the color of copper wire. Uncle presented the bird with a flourish, whisking off the newspaper cone it wore. She smiled, revealing gold teeth, and opened the door wider.

"My apprentice, Josef," Uncle said, introducing him. The boy bowed.

The woman ignored him as they entered the room and said nothing about the girl who sat on a small rug near the space heater with an open book and spiral notebook. Blue flames from the space heater reflected in her eyes and flitted along her bare arms like butterflies.

Uncle was crouping, spitting up his sleeve. The woman set the bird on a round table draped with gold fringe. Her breasts swung exposed from her kimono as she stooped to arrange it. Uncle gaped. She winked and unbuttoned his shirt, putting her ear to his wheezing chest.

"A poultice," she said, "come," leading Uncle into the kitchen.

Soon the house was full of the smell of lard and kerosene.

He stood listening to them laughing in the kitchen, watching the girl writing in the notebook.

The woman and Uncle came out arm in arm, Uncle pressing a towel to his chest. They went directly into the bedroom and closed the door.

There were new smells in the air—incense, rose water.

The girl was counting to herself, as if praying.

"I hate math," she suddenly said.

The gas-blue butterflies of the space heater fluttered across her face. The Oriental carpet she sat on had designs like scarlet moths. The wings of moths had always reminded him of Oriental carpets and he wondered if moth wings hadn't inspired them. Nature was behind every invention, Uncle had taught him.

"What's your most unfavorite subject?" she asked.

"I don't go to school anymore," he said, then realized Uncle had cautioned him never to reveal this and that the girl had already, so effortlessly, pried a secret from him. "Don't tell anyone," he said.

She smiled and made a crossed-finger sign over her lips and over her heart, where the open button of her blouse revealed budding breasts. "I can keep secrets," she said, "can you?"

The blue butterflies were whirling about the room with its buckled ceiling and cracked plaster breaking through wallpaper. The girl got up, showing her underpants as she did.

He noticed she wore small hooped earrings.

"Come in the closet," she said, then opened a door that had been wallpapered over and disappeared among coats.

"Hurry," she whispered, "before they come out."

He stood before the hanging coats. It looked like a display in a costume store—furs, boas, dressing gowns, umbrellas, the floor crowded with boots, tangled high heels, ballet slippers, galoshes.

"Where are you?" he whispered.

"Feel around."

He could smell mothballs and lavender, and tried not to remember where he'd smelled a scent like that before. He reached into the closet, filling his arms with leopard-dyed rabbit fur, buried his face in a raccoon coat, thought for an instant of telling her about the dead coons on the highway, how their guts were always the cleanest, full of crayfish at certain times of the year, but knew he should say nothing, only press into the warmth, moving toward small moans, wondering if the faint scent was hers or faded perfume the lining had absorbed forty years ago when a woman like his mother might have worn such a coat. He held the coats to him, stroking fur, kissing collars and buttons, inserting his arms up sleeves, and being kissed and fondled back, a soft voice whispering *oh Joey*. But when he tried to separate her from the fur she slipped away like a silk lining, leaving him enfolding a Persian lamb. He could hear her giggling in the depths of the closet. The bedroom door opened.

"Hey, Stefan, let's go," Uncle said.

The boy let go of the coat. The girl was nowhere to be seen. The woman slouched against the doorway of the bedroom, mascara shaping her eyes like a cat's. Her powdered breasts hung pendulous in loose fabric. Uncle reeked of kerosene and rose water, camphor, and some subtle salmon scent.

"The bird is beautiful," she said, spreading her arms within her billowy sleeves like wings so that her breasts rose nearly free of the kimono as the door closed.

They clumped down the stairs in the dark. "Remorse, remorse," Uncle kept repeating.

In the car Wolfgang growled, the engine groaned, and so did Uncle. He often groaned lately, as if oppressed by an invisible force. Groans he wasn't even aware of would build into a crescendo and everything he did would become loud—singing in a melancholy baritone, carrying on conversations with himself in strange languages, slurping soup, smacking lips, belching, farting, puffing, snorking, stomping, all accompanied by a constant droning groan.

"Dmitri, Dmitri," he groaned as they drove, "sometimes even an old man needs a mother's touch. And what about a poor boy who lives his life without it?"

⁂

The third morning after the trip to the city, they saw something they'd never seen before—the highways totally empty. They'd found little the two previous days: a dented hubcap, a flattened weasel, a torn sack at the end of a trail of lime. The boy wondered if his own dreaminess was not somehow responsible for their lack of luck.

Uncle was growing increasingly sullen, hunched behind the steering wheel, eyes squinting through cracked lenses, no longer coughing, but hardly talking either except for occasional grumbling in a foreign language. He still wore the scarf smelling of camphor and kerosene—the scents of rose water and salmon having evaporated.

"There are seasons on the highway too, Dupush," Uncle mumbled. "In spring woodchucks every few miles, in summer rabbits, coons, possum, now there should be pheasants, squirrels. We should be eating like gourmets. They must be disappointed with us at the restaurant." He swigged from the cough-medicine bottle the woman had given him. It glazed his eyes and left a sticky brown ring around his lips.

The fourth day, they arose earlier than they ever had before. Uncle said he wanted to make sure that scavengers had not invaded their territory, stripping the highways before them. Uncle made a distinction between scavengers and salvagers. He'd mounted a searchlight and swept it as they sped, alert for eyes glowing alongside the road. In the glaring headlights the highway appeared to be streaming, oil-splotched, skid-marked, and empty. Leaves gusted along curving shoulders.

At dawn, when the birches began to simmer with light, they spotted the crow. Wolfgang yelped and Uncle slammed to a gravel-skidding stop. The boy was out of the wagon before Uncle had both front wheels on the shoulder, running back toward the black body, wind inflating his burlap sack.

The crow rested on the center stripe almost too perfectly: unmarked, wings poised as if it had gently floated down in mid-flight. He stuffed it in the sack and raced back, meaning to ask Uncle if birds suffered heart attacks.

Instead of spilling the crow into the cardboard box on the backseat, Uncle examined it while the engine idled. He spread its glossy dark wings; his fingers traced its scaly feet and opened the wizened eyelids. He had to use his jackknife to pry open the beak.

"Look."

The tongue was black and split like a snake's.

"This bird talked."

"You mean like a parrot?"

"No, Dupush. Parrots gab. Crows tell secrets. This one might have told what's happening. I saw it once before. In the Old Country, just before the war. The animals all disappeared. Some said they were starting to change. There were rumors of strange animals: a fox with the face of a monkey, hares with snouts of rats, chickens with teeth. Everything was changing for the worse. And now everything is hiding again."

"From what? Another war?"

"What *another war?* You think the last one ended yet? The Nazis just moved over here. They know I know who they are. That's why they make trouble for me. Who do you think is doing these assassinations? Causing these race problems? Go back to your dreams, Nightstein."

The boy could feel himself blushing as if Uncle had caught him at something secret, and looked out the window. The first truck of the day, a semi hauling hogs, rumbled by, and the De Soto vibrated. Uncle pulled onto the road and followed it.

"They called me Nightstein too when I was your age," Uncle said in a softer voice. "I know all about it. An old woman in the village offered to buy what the priests call 'nocturnal emissions.' She thought it was sinless seed, seed a boy could spill and still be innocent. No one talks even today about a boy's innocence. It's a taboo subject, one men are ashamed of and women know nothing about, but a boy has an innocence different but as delicate as a girl's. She wanted the seed of dreams. . . . I thought I would be rich."

"What happened?"

"Nothing happened. She became a joke."

That was the last day they salvaged along the old, familiar highways. Uncle began to explore other roads, driving farther into the backcountry, narrow blacktops twisting past fiery stands of maples, highways aging into potholed, buckled, one-lane macadam, dead-ending in tarred gravel. He drove erratically, eyes continually on the rearview mirror. Black roads cut through a countryside the boy had never seen before, where the fields sank into swamp and slough and gnarled trees stood among stumps in muddy water. Autumn was absent here among cattails and willows.

They rose earlier, in the pitch-black before dawn. The riddles changed.

What is a crow?

A mortician's musician.

What is a bat?

A meat butterfly.

Animals began to appear again. Muskrats, frogs and toads, lizards, turtles, water voles. Marsh birds flapped across the highway, rasped and hooted from a camouflage of rushes. Still, many of these were animals the boy knew Uncle could salvage. But each time he signaled to stop, Uncle ignored him. Totally confused, Wolfgang began to bark, and Uncle insisted they muzzle him.

Uncle sipped steadily from the medicine bottle, his lips stained a permanent syrupy brown as if they'd been charred, eyes red-rimmed and obsessed behind greasy glasses. Whereas once he'd cursed the carelessness of other drivers, he now swerved across the road as he fiddled with the radio, dialing it far right, hunting mazurkas among crackling static.

"Why aren't we stopping for anything, Uncle?"

"It's not what we're looking for, Tadeusz."

"What are we looking for?"

"We'll know when we find it. A very special creature. One with the future in him, an animal with Wall Street ticker tape for guts, with golden ovaries, a carcass they'll pay a fortune for."

It was nearing dusk and they were driving the long drive home from the swamp roads when they found the doll. At first, because of its size and blackness, the boy thought it might be another crow. He shouted stop, wondering if they would. Uncle *had* stopped once earlier that day for a porcupine and a frazzled radiator hose, which were now in the box in the backseat. The hose had protruded from the porcupine's skull like a trunk and Uncle had braked, thinking they'd found his special animal.

"It must have been eating the hose for the salt when it got hit." Uncle had laughed when he'd seen what they'd really collected.

This time he braked so hard that Wolfgang slammed into the dashboard. The boy leaped from the wagon and ran back onto the road. She was lying staring up, arms crossed over her breast, and for the first time he understood what Uncle meant by an omen. Uncle said the feeling would simply emerge without any doubt to it and he could feel that now. The doll was a gift from the highway like the viola, but more. It was a gift he was meant to deliver to the girl.

It was a doll a girl like that could love: an elegant old woman dressed in black-crepe skirts, hatpins studded with pearls stuck about her throat like a necklace. Her skull was wisped with silver angel hair and her spidery legs ended in real shoes with spike heels and rhinestone buckles. He carefully gathered her into his sack. He could already visualize himself, dressed in his waiter's tuxedo, presenting the doll out of nowhere, like a magician. And the girl who thought his name was Joey would smile, though already he had forgotten the exact look of that smile, as if he'd worn out her image replaying it over and over.

In the wagon Uncle grabbed the sack and plucked out the doll.

"This is what you took so much time with? I thought maybe you'd found my animal for me." He tossed it into the box with the porcupine and radiator hose. She seemed to nestle in the porcupine's paws, her dress absorbing blood.

The sun was setting along a line of skeletal trees. Uncle and the boy drove in silence.

"When do you think I could start at the restaurant, Uncle?"

"She has an evil eye—did you notice? Just like in the fable."

"What fable?"

"Hah!" Uncle said to Wolfgang. "Nightstein here never heard 'The Fable of the Doll.' "

Wolfgang flattened his dragon's ears.

"Yes, yes, I know it's frightening, but then everything's frightening to you." Uncle uncorked the medicine bottle with his teeth, swigged, then began addressing the dog in a language of foreign words mixed with growls and barks, pausing to laugh uproariously as if it were a hilarious tale.

"Tell it in English, uncle."

A boy, studying to be a ventriloquist, finds a heartless-looking doll and tries to hide her. Don't ask from what. He puts her in a hatbox in the attic, but at night he hears a soprano voice repeating, "I want my heart, I want my heart!" *He goes up to the attic and when he opens the hatbox swallows swarm out from the nest they've pecked from the doll's straw. So he puts her in a steamer trunk and again he hears the voice at night and when he opens the trunk mice skitter away. They have nibbled her plaster face. So this time he locks her in a wall safe behind a huge oil painting of a ship on a stormy sea, but once again,* "I want my heart, I want my heart," *and when he opens the safe she's spilling out sawdust, crawling with carpenter ants. Things are getting worse, so at dawn he takes her to a city park near where a water fountain has become a birdbath for sparrows. He digs a rectangular hole. It's not a grave, he explains to her. He lines it with mirrors like a dressing room, and inside arranges little doll furniture all made out of mirrors—chairs, table, bureau, bookcase with mirror books, mirror candle, even a mirror bed with mirror pillows and quilt. Leaves fall; their prophecy of snow comes true. It settles deep, flat, silent. Then, at the edge of spring, with snow crusting in sunlight, when he's long forgotten the doll, he hears a muffled, screaky voice:* "My heart, my heart." *He goes to the park, still white as the train of a bridal gown, and there, everywhere, surrounding the birdbath burbling through ice, are little doll arms and little doll legs, a garden flashing with mirror rings and buckles, sprouting from the thawing earth.*

He woke from the dream. Everywhere mounted animals gazed with their glass eyes, spreading wings, varnished feathers and fur, lacquered shells, scales, teeth, claws. Along the bookshelves specimens stared from bottles. The small taxidermist-shop window was lit, but Uncle wasn't there.

He could hear Caruso singing in the basement and slowly descended the stairs. Until last year he hadn't been permitted in Uncle's workroom, but now that Uncle was teaching him to tan and preserve, it was allowed. He knew Uncle was working. Uncle always played old opera records when he worked.

The bare electric bulb dangled over the butcher block. Uncle, wearing his eyeshade, and leather apron over long underwear, was skinning the porcupine. The doll lay nearby staring at the proceedings.

He watched Uncle artfully pare meat from bone,

occasionally pausing to hose the block and toss scraps into a slop jar.

"So, Mr. Alger, you are ready to go to the big city to meet the maître d'." Uncle heaped the diced stew pieces into a marinade of bourbon.

"Do you think I'm ready, Uncle?"

"*Ridi Pagliaccio*," Uncle sang in duet with Caruso while mopping the block with operatic gestures. Then Uncle methodically spread the doll out where the porcupine had been. Paint from her face was flaked in her hair.

"Our delivery record hasn't been too hot lately. Maybe it's better to wait on the restaurant until we produce something really marvelous for them," Uncle said, sharpening his carving knife on the whetstone.

"What are you going to do with the doll?"

"How do you think she would look with the head of a porcupine stitched on?" Uncle tested the sharpness of the blade and winced. "Or how would the porcupine look with the head and dress of a doll?"

The boy wasn't totally convinced Uncle was kidding. It was getting harder to tell lately. He shook his head no.

"No good, eh?" Uncle said. "I know! I can stuff her, preserve her forever the way she looks now."

"Uncle, she's stuffed already."

"Ah! Good point. Well, what do *you* want to do with her?" he asked slyly.

"She might be rare, worth something," the boy said.

"You think she's valuable maybe? Then there's only one thing we can do."

"What's that?"

"Bury her!"

They both broke into laughter, then raced to the boxes heaped with clothing in the corner of the basement, tossing garments about as they tried on various outfits. There were full suitcases that had blown off cars, clothes that had tumbled from moving vans and laundry trucks, that had been discarded by lovers and hitchhikers, runaway clotheslines, entire wardrobes they'd picked out of branches along roadsides where abandoned farmhouses gaped, pillaged.

"How's this?" Uncle was modeling a motorcycle jacket that was ridiculously short on him, his arms sticking out. "A good Nazi jacket." He topped off his outfit with a frosted-blond wig.

The boy was enveloped by a rubber slicker he wore like a cape, a white life preserver around his neck, and a top hat they'd found one New Year's Eve.

"Don't forget the armbands, Uncle."

They tied a strip of black satin around each other's arm.

Uncle noisily sorted through piles of scrap that had accumulated against the walls. "We can bury her in this," he called, holding up a bathroom medicine cabinet, its cracked shaving mirror revealing a cardboard backing. The boy handed over the doll.

"Wolfgang! Wolfgang!" they shouted, and when the dog bounded down the stairs he was fitted with a black wreath that must have been left on the highway by a funeral cortege.

They marched up the cellar stairs, the boy with the viola, Uncle with lantern and spade, carrying the medicine chest between them.

Outside, Uncle lit the lantern and they loaded the medicine chest and spade into a wheelbarrow, then harnessed it to Wolfgang's wreath with clothesline.

"Don't trip," Uncle cautioned, raising the lantern as they picked their way. The back of the house was littered with junked cars, appliances, gutted furniture. Makeshift tombstones stuck up everywhere, marking the graves of mufflers and transmissions, the burial ground of broken radios, crates of magazines, animal bones. Ever since the game warden had confiscated his furs and equipment, and accused him of poaching, Uncle claimed he believed in keeping his valuables hidden—though, anything useful, like the viola, they dug up again a few days later.

The procession crossed a meadow, Uncle leading with the lantern, Wolfgang dragging the wheelbarrow, and the boy bringing up the rear, beating time on the drum skin of his life preserver.

They wound through an orchard that smelled faintly of fermenting apples. There was a trickle of stream he'd often played at, where morel mushrooms sprouted profusely in the spring. Uncle had brought him there to pick them long ago. His memory of that time when he first came to live with Uncle continued to be vague; it existed as a numbness the boy felt buried within him; whether unexpressed grief or love no longer mattered: he had remained faithful, even reverent to it. Uncle had once said that what had worried him most was the boy's refusing to cry. So he had tried to make the boy laugh instead, and that was something the boy could remember—Uncle holding him, rubbing a stubbly beard against his cheek, tickling him till he giggled, then whirling him upside down through the fragrance of apple blossoms. The boy was too old for that now, though they still gathered morels together in the spring. He remembered apple-picking contests, how life was when people still came to the taxidermy shop, before the game wardens had revoked Uncle's license. Uncle had refused to explain to them how he'd acquired the pelts they'd found, refused to mention anything about salvaging the highways, and once he lost his license, he became more secretive than ever. He was suspicious of everyone, convinced Kopf continued to spy on him. No one had come to visit them for a long time.

Uncle hung the lantern on a branch and began to dig, but after a few shovelfuls was so winded he had to sit down. They let Wolfgang finish, his huge paws scooping dirt between his legs. Then they lowered the medicine chest gently into the earth and covered it up. The boy knew exactly where the spot was. He'd come back in daylight and dig up the doll for the girl.

"Play a little something," Uncle requested.

The boy cradled the viola against his collar and played "Greensleeves," a bit out of tune but the only song he could play all the way through. As usual, it made Wolfgang howl.

"Ah, lovely! You can be a playing waiter. You'll make a fortune in tips, Kreisler."

The flame fluttered in the lamp and faded out. They walked back through dead leaves together in the dark.

"It was a beautiful ceremony, don't you think?" Uncle asked.

Uncle shook him from a dreamless sleep, whispering, "Wake up, Zoltán, but no light. Here, dress in your suit."

"No highways today?"

"Don't ask so much—do what your uncle tells you. And hurry."

The boy pulled on his good trousers under the quilt for warmth. Uncle's croup had returned, a smothered rattle. The man was packing the boy's clothes into a sack, huffing as if he'd been running.

"Uncle, is this an *escape?*"

"Bring your viola. Maybe they'll think it's a machine gun in the big city." Uncle chuckled. "I got mine." He opened his coat. In the dark the boy could still make out the handle of the revolver tucked in his belt.

"You dug it up!"

"Me and Wolfgang. Digging all night while you snored, Nightstein," Uncle explained as they moved through the darkened house. It seemed nearly stripped. Places where the boy instinctively balanced to bump past end tables were now only empty spaces. The stuffed animals that had loomed from walls and shelves—moosehead, antlers, hawks, owls—were gone. "Hidden away like a squirrel's acorns," Uncle whispered. "When they come this time it will be just another abandoned house. Here."

Uncle handed him a change purse. The boy could feel the weight of coins in it among crushed bills.

"What's this for?"

"You never know," Uncle said. "Something might happen to me. In case we get separated."

Uncle had never given him money during any of their other escapes. Nor had he ever hidden things so thoroughly. Usually, the escapes were more like drills. Uncle would wake him in the middle of the night saying that Kopf was on the way, or the truant officer, or the dogcatcher, the Gestapo, the KKK, sometimes never exactly who. They would sneak from the house with their coats on over their nightclothes and ride around the back roads until Uncle felt it was safe to return home.

"I don't want us to get separated, Uncle."

"It's always best to be prepared. Besides, I thought you were ready to go work at the restaurant."

"Just to *work* there. I didn't mean to live there."

Uncle hugged him in the dark, empty taxidermy shop. "Don't worry, Dupush, you can live off the land. You're ready for anything."

The boy could still smell the faint camphor scent about the old man, mixed with cigar smoke and the odd, herbal odor of the cough medicine. It reminded him of the night with the girl, of returning to the city where she lived, and of the doll he'd wanted to give her—there wasn't time now to dig it up. The doll would have to wait under the orchard until he got back. He wished they were merely going out to salvage. He'd never enjoyed the escape drills.

Uncle disconnected the little doorbell and they sneaked to where the De Soto was parked under birch trees. Wolfgang was already inside, shivering and wagging, wedging his head out from under the seat to lick their faces. Up close the boy could see that Uncle had not buried everything. The back of the wagon was stuffed with specimens—all the large birds and foxes, the lynx, antlers, a jumbled menagerie. The moosehead had been roped to the carriers on the roof of the car.

"Look what they did," Uncle said, striking a match along the side of the station wagon. Finger-etched in the dirt on the door was a swastika.

They drove onto the interstate, toward the city, away from their usual routes. Semis passed, towing clattering, empty automobile trailers, diesel horns bellowing as their headlights illuminated the moosehead. Uncle kept exhorting the boy to see if they were being followed, convinced that Kopf, still suspecting them of poaching, would tail them into the city, trying to uncover Uncle's outlets for illegal furs and game.

"Those headlights have been following us all the way, haven't they, Zoltán?"

The boy tried to stay alert, but kept drowsing. As sometimes happened late at night, Uncle couldn't seem to stop talking, rambling from one subject to another, connecting facts in a web of increasingly distorted stories: Kopf's persecution of him, their hard luck on the highways, the blank road and evil omens—strange animals, the doll, how if one were to dig her up there'd be nothing but one's own reflection staring back from the earth, and how earlier that evening, after the burial, while trying to pick up Caruso singing faintly among the ghosts of polka stations, he'd tuned in on the sound of crows.

"Crows—they were on the radio. When I heard them I knew it was time to get the hell out. We'll try the city."

All the while Uncle talked the boy fought sleep, jerking awake from half dreams confused with Uncle's phantoms: a recurring sensation of headlights passing through his body, of lead-soled running across railroad tracks to a highway where trucks rumbled in the white smoke of snow and he walked backward along the shoulder, hitchhiking in the exit-sign aura of flares.

He opened his eyes to a gray sky and pale streetlights

still burning. They were cruising down a deserted street of apartment buildings, lined with parked cars, fog condensed on their windshields. Uncle, silent and haggard, turned into an alley.

"The restaurant?" the boy asked. He suddenly didn't want to see it in the daylight.

"No. I just wanted to lose anybody following us. Besides, we couldn't show up at the restaurant empty-handed after missing deliveries all week saying, 'All right, get the tuxedo out for the kid.' We need something special for them." Uncle's voice was very hoarse.

They turned back onto a street. The boy knew the lighter it got, the more outlandish they looked. On top, beside the moosehead, Uncle had tied a lacrosse stick they'd once found poking from a beaver dam. In the backseat, Wolfgang sat perfectly still as if trying to blend in with the postured animals he was surrounded with. People, waiting on corners for buses to take them to work, stared as they drove by. Uncle tried to hum "The Song of the Volga Boatman" and began to hack. The boy sank down in his seat with the uneasy feeling that Uncle was driving aimlessly.

"A couple DPs with nowhere to call home, eh?" Uncle said.

They were on an expressway in heavy traffic, crossing a suspension bridge over the river. Uncle turned off at the next exit, down a street of factories with broken windows, past towering grain elevators, where they bumped over railroad tracks, and finally down a cinder road winding among scrap yards. There were no longer any buildings. The skyline, in an industrial haze, rose jagged beyond the fields and river. But what dominated the boy's attention was the black railroad bridge they were driving toward. He'd noticed it downriver when they crossed the suspension bridge, and it had appeared massive even at that distance.

"What's it look like?" Uncle asked.

"Giant wings."

"A Black Angel. Though some call it the Jackknife because of how it opens."

Uncle parked the wagon off the rutted trail that had deteriorated to two muddy treads impressed by enormous tires. Payscrapers and bulldozers rusted in fields like grazing prehistoric animals. Everything seemed gigantic and abandoned here. The boy felt vulnerable and vaguely afraid, but Uncle was grinning.

"How do you feel about climbing it?" he asked.

"The bridge! For what?"

"Pigeon eggs."

They trampled toward the river through dry, blond weeds, dragging Wolfgang along on a clothesline leash.

"We might need him to scare off some of the maniacs around here," Uncle said.

A freight train was clattering across the bridge, open boxcar doors making it look abandoned too. Thousands of glinting birds glided about its spans.

Uncle pointed. "A sky full of squab."

They followed a streambed lined with rusted cans and bottles. Rabbits bounced off; a hen pheasant broke. Despite the acrid breeze of chemicals and sewage the area seemed a wilderness, secret at the very heart of the city.

The bank curved by a blue mound of salt. Beneath the collapsed framework of an old wooden trestle stood a charred boxcar, its stovepipe chimney knocked askew, rough-cut windows and doors blackened.

"Goddamn!" Uncle said. "They burned out Cookie John."

"Who?"

"Always questions with you, Dupush. Cookie John. A tramp. A squatter. An old friend. Who does these things? It's always the same—other tramps, a gang of boys, *polici*, railroad dicks, some kind of Nazis!" Uncle sat down heavily and began to shake with coughing, gasping for breath between attacks. It brought tears to his eyes. When it was over he looked very old and drained in the bright sunlight.

"Uncle, I'm sorry. Sometimes I'm not sure what's real and what's a joke anymore."

"*Everything* used to be real to you, Dupush. Now you're starting to sort it out. Someday, when you understand about death, you'll answer your own question. Either everything's real or nothing's real. There's no in-between. People who find an in-between live foolish lives."

Uncle stood. Wolfgang's muscles were twitching as if he were being swarmed by invisible flies. They had to tug him the rest of the way to the bridge, his hind legs dragging as if still broken. Uncle tied him to one of the dwarfed willows that grew horizontally out of the bank. A small rowboat, coated in a gray film of mud, had been pulled up among the trees on the narrow slope of shore. The dog began to whimper as they climbed in and Uncle shoved them off.

"Tell him something soothing," Uncle said.

"We'll be right back," the boy told the dog. "Don't worry."

But Wolfgang continued to strain at the leash, snapping back on it, dancing up on his hind legs.

Uncle poled them around the huge concrete abutment with a long pole, hooked at one end like a shepherd's crook, while the boy tried to paddle with a stubby oar that seemed better suited as a ladle. The river smelled of tar, like a hot highway. It flowed sluggishly, feculent, a surface of oil slicks and brown suds. Water seeped into the bottom of the boat and he tried not to get his shoes wet; Uncle said men had died from letting it come in contact with an open sore. Wolfgang was barking wildly from shore.

"Well, anybody interested knows we're here now,"

Uncle said. "I should have bit off his tail. That's what happens when you let their tails grow. Keep an eye open for railroad dicks. They carry pepper guns."

"What's that?"

"Shotguns loaded with rock salt instead of buckshot."

They had floated under the deep shadows of the bridge and it was suddenly chilly. The boy looked up through the black, ponderous latticework of beams and trusses, railroad track and spans, semaphores, and flame-blue autumn sky leaking light through uncountable angles. From below, the structure of the bridge made no sense at all. Uncle hooked a rusty rung in the concrete and moored the boat, and they clambered up the rung ladder.

The girders were just wide enough to walk on, studded with rivets, slippery with grease and crusted pigeon droppings. The boy felt clumsy climbing in his suit, trying to keep it clean. They climbed level by level, ascending a series of narrow metal ladders. The river flowed torpidly below, though the higher they climbed, the more it sparkled. He could see circles bursting on the surface almost as if fish, impossibly alive in the poisoned current, were feeding. Wind twanged in the overhead struts.

"Where are the nests?"

"In the upper girders, tucked in the trusses." Uncle still carried the long, hooked pole, using it to boost himself along. He was breathing heavily, wheezing, and when they reached the railroad tracks he had to stop to catch his breath.

"I can't make it further, Zoltán. You have to get up there alone from here. They're out there over the middle of the river. Here, take this." Uncle handed him a sack shaped like a wind sock, made from cheesecloth like a butterfly net. "Put the eggs in this. Be very careful," Uncle cautioned, mussing the boy's hair.

The ladders had ended. He climbed the latticework of

girders that rose over the tracks in towering, cantilevered wings, glancing back at each level for Uncle's hand signals. The tar smell of the river had been replaced by a smell of the bridge itself—of grease, corrosion, iron, and damp feathers. Finally, at the proper height, Uncle, far below, directed him out over the river. The boy inched along a girder, peeking down, though trying not to, at the shimmering, increasingly narrow-looking river. He'd never been higher. The entire city spread out in a haze. He breathed deeply and allowed himself the view.

Noon patinaed the downtown skyscrapers. Smokestacks fumed among copper green church steeples and an endless assortment of water towers. Overhead, an airliner droned, and he wondered if anyone could see him—a boy on a bridge with a white sack blowing like a pennant. His mind seemed clearer than it ever had before, as if he were seeing in a new way. His life spread out before him like the cityscape, suspended in time, rather than the dark, speeding blur it had been on the highways. This was a landscape he was the center of, completely alone, though surrounded by a city. The dreams were over. Out there under plumes of smoke in some glinting neighborhood the girl sat in a classroom over a math book. Between them was a distance greater than between foreign countries. He could actually *see* from the bridge that in escaping to the city Uncle had merely substituted one kind of isolation for another. And with an intensity of feeling that surprised him, he knew that it didn't matter if the doll in the orchard were ever dug up—he would never see the girl again. The doll had been his first omen, but he had misinterpreted it. Rather than a gift the doll was a warning. It was the burial, not the doll, that had meaning. The doll could have been anything—a shoe, a hubcap, a bottle. His mind had never put things together so easily. Uncle had kept telling him there would be a breakthrough, that insight would come in a flash, and even as the boy began to understand he wanted the understanding to stop, wanted to tell Uncle he didn't want any more experience with omens. It was better to live without them than to be so wrong, than to realize suddenly as he just had that the girl was no more possible than the restaurant for which he had climbed a bridge to gather pigeon eggs.

He started back along the girder, looking for Uncle below, wanting to signal that he was coming down. But Uncle was no longer there.

A gust of wind almost knocked him off balance. Between gusts an eerie cooing reverberated like waves of a tuning fork. From where he stood he could survey the length of the bridge. Leaning out over the river, he glimpsed the rowboat still moored to the abutment, but couldn't spot Wolfgang among the scrub trees along the bank. Pigeons flapped like laundry among the girders. Inflated males strutted along beams, swiveling iridescent heads. He began finding nests tucked in the latticed trusses—ancient-looking constructions of weeds, rags, foil, paper. The pigeons are salvagers too, he thought. He couldn't resist gathering eggs. Panicked birds flailed past his head as he reached into nests. The footing was treacherous with droppings, but he continued edging farther out over the river, toward the opposite shore, plundering the small white eggs, handfuls splattering on the girders and tumbling through updrafts as he angrily stuffed the sack.

He was more than halfway to the other side when he heard the first shot. It boomed amplified through the superstructure, launching flurries of birds like secondary explosions. The boy grabbed a girder and held on as they beat around him. He frantically scanned the bridge for Uncle, spotting two men instead, approaching from below, jogging along the railroad tracks. He glanced from them back across the river, checking for the De Soto. It was still there, windshield flaring on a rise beyond the blue mountain of salt. From the bridge the station wagon appeared the size of a toy, but he could clearly make out the black-and-white markings of the squad car parked beside it.

"Uncle," he tried yelling, "Uncle," but his voice was swept away by wind. Another shot propelled the birds into frenetic circles. Its echoes ricocheted among the girders so that he couldn't tell what direction it had come from. The *polici* on the tracks dropped to a crouch. He could see their blue uniforms but not whether they'd drawn their guns. They didn't seem to be doing the shooting.

Bells were ringing insistently upriver and down. He tried to move but his legs were locked and his hands clutched a girder in a knuckle-aching grip. A horn blasted, its deep vibration traveling the iron beams into his bones. A floating junkyard was moving toward the bridge—cabled barges heaped with scrap cars, pushed by a tug. He felt a rumbling tremor and slid to his knees as the landscape began to tilt. The bridge was opening.

Pigeons continued to wheel, gulls, starlings, and grackles screaming in their midst. The two *polici* on the tracks, trying to scramble back before the bridge opened completely, lunged to either side as Wolfgang, clothesline streaming, hurtled past them. The dog's rangy body compressed and expanded with each pumping stride, and as if possessed by terror and his own velocity, he leaped the gap between the expanding black spans of the bridge, arcing slow-motion through midair, and for a moment the boy thought the dog might make it, then he looked away as Wolfgang plunged.

When the boy opened his eyes barges were passing below. He began working hand over hand down the elevated girders toward the base of the bridge, using the rivets as toe holds. His suit was torn, grease-slathered, smeared with yolk and feathers from the egg sack he'd knotted to his belt. Tears were running down his face though he didn't feel that he was crying. He felt numb—the bridge was too massive for tears to mean anything. Across the gulf of its gaping wings he saw where Uncle had been hiding from the *polici*. Crouched in the latticework of girders beneath the railroad tracks, Uncle was gesturing wildly to him. Sunlight flashed off the revolver in Uncle's hand, and the boy guessed it had been Uncle firing earlier in an effort to attract his attention to the barges before the bridge opened. Uncle continued to signal. The barges with their mangled autos slid like endless highway wrecks beneath thousands of screeching, birds. Warning bells clanged. Finally the boy raised his arm. Through swirling birds he waved good-bye.

Made in the USA
Coppell, TX
23 December 2020